THE MYSTERY OF THE DISAPPEARING DOGS

GHOST TWINS

THE MYSTERY OF THE DISAPPEARING DOGS

Dian Curtis Regan

AN
APPLE
PAPERBACK

SCHOLASTIC INC.
New York Toronto London Auckland Sydney

No part of this publication may be reproduced in whole or in part, or stored in a retrieval system, or transmitted in any form or by any means, electronic, mechanical, photocopying, recording, or otherwise, without written permission of the publisher. For information regarding permission, write to Scholastic Inc., 555 Broadway, New York, NY 10012.

ISBN 0-590-25241-0

12 11 10 9 8 7 6 5 4 3 2   5 6 7 8 9/9 0/0

Printed in the U.S.A.   40

First Scholastic printing, May 1995

For Erin McCormack

Contents

Tuesday, **August 25, 1942**   *5 cents*

JUNIPER DAILY NEWS

New Fall Fashions Inside!

Twins Involved in Boating Mishap

Robert Adam Zuffel and his twin sister, Rebeka Allison, seem to be victims of a boating accident at Kickingbird Lake. Their dog, Thatch, disappeared with them. Family members say that the twins had gone hiking on Mystery Island and were probably returning when yesterday's windstorm blew in.

Their overturned canoe was floating in the water off Mystery Island. A party of family members searched the lake and the surrounding area, but no trace of the twins or their dog was found.

Today's Highlights

President Roosevelt Welcomes Cary Grant to White House . . pg.2

Zoot Suits All the Rage pg.3

Movie Review: *Bambi* pg.5

Local Student Wins Award for Model of All 48 States pg.6

THE MYSTERY OF THE DISAPPEARING DOGS

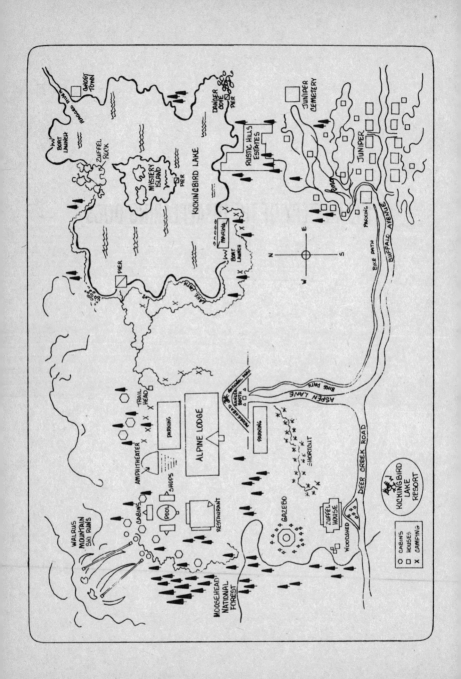

1
What Was in the Backyard

"**I** can't hold him much longer!"

Robbie watched in amusement while Beka, his twin sister, struggled to keep Thatch away from the attic window so the ghost dog wouldn't see what was in the backyard.

What was in the backyard was a *dog*. A *real* dog!

A dog who'd arrived at the Zuffel house this morning, along with her owners — a young honeymooning couple from New Jersey.

The old house at Kickingbird Lake Resort was a vacation rental, but it used to be the home of the Zuffel twins. Now the twins haunted the house, along with Thatch, the ghost dog.

Thatch's house had not only been invaded by

1

another dog, but by another St. Bernard — who looked just like him, only smaller, with a milky-white neck and cinnamon patches of fur swirling around each eye and across both flanks.

Thatch whined and barked and panted.

Robbie was glad the window wasn't open, or his dog might leap three stories to the ground. Of course, to a ghost dog, that wouldn't be a problem.

Beka made a face at Thatch's whining. "Gosh, Rob, he's having a cat fit!"

When Thatch heard the word "cat," his paws began to race in place.

"Don't say C-A-T!" Robbie yelped, lunging to grasp the dog's collar. "He *knows* that word."

Beka laughed, hopping aside to let her brother take over.

"It's not funny." Now Robbie was wrestling with Thatch on the hardwood floor to distract him.

His sister peered out the window. "Hey, they're playing catch. With a green tennis ball."

"Thanks for the afternoon news report," Robbie mumbled, ducking Thatch's wet kisses.

"What a beautiful dog," Beka exclaimed.

"*Grr-yip!*" said Thatch.

"Oh, not as beautiful as you, puppy." Beka knelt to hug him. "You're the most beautiful dog *not* in this world."

It was Robbie's turn to laugh — at the truth in his sister's words.

"Raz," Beka began, calling him by their shared initials. "We can't keep him locked up for a whole week."

"You're right." Robbie loosened his grip on Thatch. "But he's making me nervous. Who knows what he might do? At least the other dog's a *female*. That might keep Thatch from getting too upset."

"Whoever heard of taking a dog on your honeymoon?" Beka groaned, rolling her eyes.

"Whoever heard of naming a dog *Madison?*" Robbie added.

"Oh, I *like* the name. I heard the lady call her *Maddie* for short."

In two paw steps, Thatch was up in the window seat, dragging Robbie along with him.

Robbie sighed. "Might as well go downstairs and get this over with." He covered both ears to block the doggie noises. "I just hope Thatch doesn't scare away our new guests."

Robbie pondered his own words. When people first started coming to stay in the Zuffel house, the twins *wanted* to scare them away.

But every family brought new adventures. Now the twins looked forward to renters filling the house with light and noise — and *food*. (For a

3

ghost, an occasional snack was a treat, especially for a ghost *dog*!)

The twins hustled across the attic and down two flights of stairs to the kitchen. The back door was propped open, letting late spring warmth and fresh air into the house — which had been shut up for several weeks between renters.

Thatch didn't need a special invitation. With the twins on his tail, he burst out the door, off the cedar deck, and across the yard.

The honeymooning couple didn't know that two kids and a dog had just popped out of their vacation home and were dashing toward them.

But their dog knew.

Maddie put on the brakes. The tennis ball sailed over her head and *thwacked* into the bushes next to the gazebo.

"You missed," hollered the lady. She trotted after the ball.

"Hey, Madison," the man called. "What's wrong, girl?"

Maddie looked like a dog statue, motionless, nose lifted. The only thing moving were her eyes.

And her muscles. Robbie could see them tensing under her fur, as if she was ready to take flight.

"Oh, Mrs. Shelby," the man called in a singsongy voice. "Come look."

His wife giggled at being called by her new married name. "Coming, Mr. Shelby." She snatched the ball from the bushes and dashed back, pausing to kneel by the dog. "Are you okay?"

Maddie took three steps backward.

Mainly because Thatch had taken three steps *toward* her.

"She looks as though she's seen a ghost," Mrs. Shelby exclaimed.

"Ha," Robbie answered. "You couldn't be more correct."

With a playful yelp, Thatch bounded around the girl dog.

Robbie was relieved. *Playful bounding* was fine. *Angry charging* was not. Maybe Thatch just wanted to play — not drive the dog away.

"Look at him," Beka said, circling the yard to get a better look.

Thatch touched noses with Maddie, then gallumphed away, like an overgrown puppy. Tearing back, he rolled onto his back, kicking his legs in the air, as though he welcomed a playmate.

"Not to worry," Robbie said. "He *likes* her."

Beka watched Thatch's antics. "I don't think so."

"What do you mean? He's not tearing her to shreds. That *must* mean he likes her."

"Thatch is acting *way* too goofy." Beka sat on the grass, cocking her head to study the dogs. "I think what we have here is a classic case of puppy love."

Robbie groaned. Could his sister be right?

2
Watcher in the Shadows

Robbie was amazed.
    After Maddie's initial shock over the presence of the ghost dog, she relaxed. Not only relaxed — she began to *play* with Thatch!

"Can she *see* him?" Beka asked, sitting beside Robbie on the deck.

"I don't know." That question had entered Robbie's mind many times since he first realized he was a ghost. Could people sometimes see them?

There'd been rumors among townspeople about "faces at the attic windows" of the old Zuffel house. The attic was where they spent most of their time.

Did Maddie have a sixth sense?

Or, did the ghost dog *do* something? Did he

7

"open a window" between the two worlds, allowing Maddie to see him?

Thatch always discovered new "ghost rules" before they did. He'd been first to *smoosh* — zip through tiny openings, like keyholes. Plus, he'd taught them how to reach from "their world" into "this world" and make things move.

The Shelbys headed inside to eat dinner — sandwiches dropped off by a delivery girl from Blaze's Burgers in the nearby town of Juniper.

Pieces of the couple's conversation floated out to Robbie's ears.

". . . acting strange," Mr. Shelby was saying about Maddie.

"Almost as if she's playing with another dog," his wife added. "Did your brother give us a *faulty* wedding gift?"

"Of course not." The man sounded offended. "Madison was the pick of the litter."

"Then why did he give her away?"

"You know why; she was outgrowing his house and yard."

"Is that a nice way of saying she was eating him out of house and home?" the lady teased.

"Uh-oh," Robbie said. "The honeymooners are having their first argument."

Beka got up to peek into the kitchen. "You call this arguing?"

Robbie's curiosity made him join her. Between bites of Blaze's famous corned beef on rye with homemade sauerkraut, the couple traded kisses.

"Ewww," Robbie said, wrinkling his nose.

Beka gave him a playful punch.

"Madison is a *wonderful* wedding gift," Mrs. Shelby said. "But if we can't find a dog-sitter, I don't know how we're going to do all the fun things we wanted to do this week."

"There must be plenty of kids around," her husband said. "Like him."

Robbie jumped. *Him?* Could the man see him leaning against the door frame, eavesdropping?

But Mr. Shelby was pointing beyond Robbie, out toward the sugarberry grove which circled the gazebo.

"Look!" Beka cried at the same instant.

Robbie squinted into the early evening shadows.

A boy hunched among the trees, moving as though he didn't want to be seen. He was watching the dogs. Of course he could see only *one* dog — Maddie.

Mr. Shelby dropped his sandwich and hurried outside.

The twins scuttled out of his way.

"Hey!" he called, waving at the boy. "Come here."

The boy froze. With a guilty glance in their direction, he melted into the trees and disappeared.

"You must have startled him," his wife said, stepping onto the deck.

Mr. Shelby batted away a fluttering moth. "Maybe he thought I was going to bawl him out for trespassing." Picking up the tennis ball from the side of the step, he tossed it to Maddie.

Thatch leaped for it, but Maddie snatched it away.

"Whew," Robbie muttered, glad Thatch hadn't made the ball "disappear" while everyone was watching.

"If the boy comes back," Mr. Shelby said, "I'll offer him a job — watching out for Maddie while we play tourists."

A faint ringing echoed from the entry hall.

"Someone's at the front door." Mrs. Shelby hurried through the kitchen.

"Mr. Tavolott?" Beka offered.

Mr. Tavolott was the owner of Kickingbird Lake Resort. He often dropped in on new renters to make sure everything was okay.

"I didn't hear his jeep come up the drive," Robbie said.

Curious, he followed Mrs. Shelby through the house to the tiled entry hall with the high ceiling.

A stairway with an oak banister curved down from the second floor.

A girl about his age — eleven — stood on the veranda. The sides of her dark hair were pulled back with a poofy green bow. A collie dog "smiled" from the front of her matching green shirt.

Robbie recognized her. He'd seen her at the library in Juniper, where the twins "checked out" books, or curled up to read on rainy afternoons when the house was empty and lonely.

"Excuse me," she said politely. "I'm looking for my dog. She's missing." The sad-faced girl thrust a picture toward Mrs. Shelby.

Robbie stepped close to look.

Mrs. Shelby shivered. "Oh, my, the temperature must be dropping. Would you come inside for a minute?"

The girl moved into the entry hall and closed the door.

Mrs. Shelby shivered again, as if the closed door didn't help.

"Sorry," Robbie said, knowing *he'd* caused the "drop in temperature." It was one of his *ghost traits* he often forgot about.

Robbie studied the picture of the girl's pets. Two golden retrievers, with fur the color of molasses taffy.

"What lovely dogs," said Mrs. Shelby. "What are their names?"

"Shawnee and Luka," the girl said. "Shawnee disappeared two days ago. I think someone *stole* her because she'd *never* run away from Luka."

"Goodness." Mrs. Shelby handed back the picture. "We just arrived today, but I promise to keep an eye out for your dog."

"Thank you." The girl started to open the door.

"By the way," Mrs. Shelby added quickly. "Would you be interested in pet-sitting *our* dog?"

A smile washed the sadness from the girl's face. "Sure! I have my own pet-sitting service. With twelve clients." She began to count on her fingers: "Five dogs, three cats, one parrot, two horses, one hamster."

"And a par-tri-idge in a pear tree . . ." Beka sang, making Robbie laugh.

"What kind of dog do you have?" the girl asked.

"Come on, I'll show you."

Mrs. Shelby led the way to the deck. Thatch and Maddie were still frolicking on the lawn — only it looked as though Maddie was alone, chasing an imaginary friend.

"This is . . ." Mrs. Shelby paused.

"Alix," the girl answered. "I live in Juniper. My dad is Mr. Silver, the postmaster."

"Pleased to meet you, Alix Silver." Mr. Shelby shook her hand. "We wanted to go to a movie in about an hour, but didn't want to leave Maddie alone in an unfamiliar house. Would you keep her company?"

"I'll ask my dad," she told them. Flying out the door, she stopped briefly to introduce herself to Maddie, and give her a few quick hugs. And then she dashed down the road to Juniper.

"Yeah, we have a dog-sitter!" Mrs. Shelby cheered.

"Which means, we also have a *date*," her husband answered, swooping her into his arms.

Robbie pretended to gag. "You two had better finish your sandwiches," he warned.

"If not," Beka added, "they'll be gobbled down by a hungry ghost dog."

The Shelbys returned to the kitchen table, almost as if they'd heard the twins' warning.

As Robbie started to follow them inside, his eyes caught a movement in the trees.

"What is it?" Beka whispered, following his gaze.

"It's him again," Robbie whispered back.

The boy they'd spotted earlier was still there, stealing through the sugarberry grove.

Watching and waiting.

For what?

Robbie's sense of protecting his own territory was as strong as Thatch's. No way would he let this boy get away with trespassing.

He'd find out who the guy was, what he wanted — and why he was using the cover of twilight and trees to keep from being seen.

3
The Dognapper

Two hours later, Robbie sprawled on the floor of the family room, petting Thatch, who lay exhausted on the fireplace rug after the wild romp with his new playmate.

Maddie lay next to him. One paw overlapped Thatch's, meaning it went *through* the ghost dog's paw.

On the sofa sat Alix, reading a book about dogs while Beka read over her shoulder.

"This girl is *really* into dogs," Beka said.

"Aha!" Alix slid from the sofa to the floor next to Maddie. "Here's a picture that looks just like you."

Robbie quickly rolled to one side to get out of the girl's way. Having a person take up the same space as you felt funny — like a blown-up balloon inside of you.

Alix showed the page to Maddie. The dog's eyes opened to watch what the girl was doing, then closed again. Thatch must have worn *Maddie* out.

"It says," Alix read, "A St. Bernard is a smart dog with a keen sense of smell." She scanned the rest of the article. "You're famous for rescuing people. Hundreds of years ago, you helped monks find lost travelers in the Swiss Alps."

She turned a page. "And it says you're an excellent guide, and can warn travelers of dangerous footing. Plus, you're a loyal watchdog."

"We knew that," Beka said, jutting out her chin, acting proud of Thatch.

Alix flipped through the book. "Here's a picture of *my* dogs." She held the page so Maddie could see the golden retrievers, but Maddie didn't care to look.

"My dogs are smart, too. They're good hunting dogs. Shawnee and Luka are sisters." Alix closed the book and set it aside. "I miss Shawnee." Her voice wavered. "Why would someone take her?"

Robbie felt sad, too. He didn't know Shawnee, but he knew how he'd feel if Thatch disappeared.

Behind Alix's back, Beka rested her hand on the dog book, concentrating, until she could move the cover, meaning now it was in her power.

Robbie watched her open the book. "What are you doing?"

"I wasn't finished reading," she explained. "There's a story in here about a famous dog named Barry, who rescued forty people lost on a mountain in Switzerland."

"Was he a St. Bernard?" Robbie asked.

"Of course." She gave him a smug grin.

Maddie came to her feet, almost as if she was reacting to Beka's story. "Oh, don't be jealous of Barry," Beka teased. "*You* could've rescued those people, too."

The dog padded toward the kitchen.

"Do you need to go outside?" Alix scrambled to her feet, stepping over the book. Pausing, she gave it a puzzled look, as if she clearly remembered closing it. Reaching down, she flipped it shut, then hurried after Maddie to take her outside.

Robbie stretched. "I'm off to the attic. Are you coming?"

"Be right there," Beka told him. She opened the book again and continued to read.

Robbie resisted the urge to stay and see Alix's reaction to the open book after shutting it twice. "Thatch?" he called. "Ready for bed?"

The dog groaned in answer, shifting to a more comfortable spot, making it clear he intended to stay right where he was.

"Thatch got more exercise than normal today," Robbie said. "We may need to take him to the lake tomorrow to revive him."

Beka agreed.

Kickingbird Lake held the source of their strength. Whenever they overtired themselves, or wandered too far from the area, they felt their energy drain. A trip to the lake quickly brought them back "to normal."

Robbie headed upstairs "to bed."

Ghosts didn't need to sleep. But, since everyone else went off to bed at night, they did, too.

The attic bedroom was as comfortable as an old pair of worn slippers. It was the only space in the Zuffel house "belonging" to them. Not many visitors ventured to the attic, and when they did, the twins did their best to scare them away.

Robbie sat on the bunk bed. He'd claimed the lower bunk, and Beka and Thatch had taken the top — more than fifty years ago!

Nights passed quickly once he lay down and closed his eyes, even though what he did was more like "floating" than sleeping.

Before Robbie could get comfortable, something made him get up to check on Alix and Maddie in the backyard.

From his view at the window, Robbie could see the dog sniffing here and there while Alix waited.

CLUNK!

Robbie flinched. What was that? Something heavy had hit the side of the house.

He glanced below to see if Alix had heard it.

She was dashing across the yard and around the house to investigate. Before Robbie could move to do the same, his gaze landed on a figure racing across the lawn toward Maddie.

It was the mystery boy who was snooping around earlier.

The boy tossed something toward Maddie. She dove for it as though it were prime rib.

While Maddie wolfed down the treat, the boy snapped a leash onto her collar.

In a flash, he hurried the dog toward the cover of dark trees and disappeared.

4

The Chase

Stunned, Robbie's eyes stayed locked upon the dark line of trees until he glimpsed two figures rushing down the shortcut from the backyard to Aspen Lane.

The boy must have thrown a rock at the side of the house to make Alix leave the yard. He'd this whole *dognapping* scheme planned!

Robbie raced downstairs.

Beka met him on her way to the kitchen. "Did you hear a loud noise?"

"Yes!" He didn't have time to stop and explain. "Come on; we've got to catch him."

"Catch *who?*" Beka called, racing after him.

In the kitchen, the twins came to a screeching stop.

The door was closed.

Closed door and ghosts don't mix.

"Rats," Robbie mumbled.

But before he had time to go to *Plan B*, the door burst open.

A white-faced Alix rushed *through* him.

Robbie cringed.

"MADDIE!" Alix hollered.

Her answer was silence.

She wrung her hands. "Oh, what am I thinking? The door was *shut;* Maddie couldn't have come in." Her words tumbled out so fast, they sounded garbled.

With an abrupt turn, Alix tore outside again.

The twins didn't hesitate. In two steps they were out the door, and across the yard.

"He went this way!" Robbie hollered before his sister could ask what they were doing.

Alix stayed in the yard, making large circles as she called, "Maddie! Where are you?"

The twins rushed through the sand plum trees which lined the shortcut.

Before they were halfway to the road, a dog was on their heels, barking like crazy.

At first Robbie thought it was Maddie, then he noticed moonlight glimmering through the racing figure.

It was Thatch, who'd sprung to life again.

"How'd *he* know something was wrong?" Robbie hurried along, impressed with his "smart dog with a keen sense of smell." He wondered if Thatch knew something awful had happened to Maddie. Or if he sensed she might be in danger.

They broke through the trees onto Aspen Lane. The valley, washed in moonlight, was breathtaking. Robbie was thankful for the light, yet it showed him a deserted road.

"He could have headed south toward Juniper, or north into Moosehead," Robbie grumbled.

"Or *east* toward Kickingbird Lake," Beka added. She tapped Robbie on the shoulder. "Excuse me, Raz, may I ask a simple question?"

Robbie nodded, annoyed at himself for not knowing which direction to search.

"Who is the HE that we're chasing? And what did HE do?"

Robbie quickly filled her in on what he'd witnessed from the attic window.

"Wow."

Beka's hazy outline shimmered in the dim light, almost as if she was woven from moonbeams.

The effect was nifty. Robbie wondered if he looked the same to her.

"Might as well head back," he finally said, feeling a mixture of disappointment over losing the dognapper, and worry over Maddie's safety.

"Alix is probably beside herself by now," Beka said. "How will she explain to the Shelbys that she lost their dog?"

"Ewww." Robbie was glad he wasn't in Alix's shoes, yet he knew it wasn't the girl's fault. If only he could tell the Shelbys what *really* happened.

Robbie headed into the trees. "We've got to find that boy and follow him. I have a strange feeling he has something to do with Shawnee's disappearance, too."

"I agree." Beka stepped down the moon-shadowed shortcut. "Come on, Thatch," she called.

They both froze as the realization hit them at the same instant.

"Thatch!" Robbie shouted.

Rushing back to the road, he peered frantically in both directions. Thatch could have easily picked up Maddie's scent — and followed her.

"Did you see which way he — ?"

"Nope," Beka said. "Sorry. I was too busy listening to your story about the . . . the dognapping. I forgot Thatch was with us."

They both fell silent, watching and listening.

"Thatch could have taken off in any direction," Beka said. "Even back through the shortcut. I doubt the dognapper stayed on the road. He'd be too easy to spot."

Robbie kicked a tree stump. First he let the *boy* get away, and now, Thatch. "Well, Thatch will come home. Unfortunately, *he'll* know where Maddie is, and we won't."

The twins jogged back through the shortcut.

Robbie's *biggest* worry was that Thatch *wouldn't* come back.

Now that the dog had found his first playmate in fifty years, wouldn't he rather stay with her?

5
Thatch's Night Out

Beka was right.
By the time they returned to the house, Alix was close to tears.

She was sitting on the back steps, head in her hands. "How could this happen?" she was mumbling. "Watching dogs is my *business*. What am I going to tell the Shelbys?"

On cue, the sound of voices and footsteps echoed from the front of the house.

Alix leaped to her feet and dashed inside.

The twins slipped through the door before it slammed, following Alix to meet the Shelbys in the entry hall.

The couple's light conversation ended abruptly when they saw the girl's tear-streaked face.

"What happened? Are you all right? Where's Maddie?"

The questions came faster than Alix could answer them.

"Mr. and Mrs. Shelby, *please* don't be mad at me. I was taking really good care of Maddie, and . . . and . . ." With a deep breath, Alix quickly told them what had happened.

Mrs. Shelby hugged Alix to calm her down. "Maybe the dog wandered off into the trees, and can't find her way back," she offered. "Maddie's unfamiliar with her surroundings."

"No, she *couldn't* have wandered off," Alix told them. "I think she was *taken.*"

The grown-ups exchanged glances.

"Alix," Mr. Shelby began. "The chances of someone kidnapping our dog are — "

"But I have evidence," Alix blurted.

Robbie felt sorry for the girl. The Shelbys obviously didn't believe her.

"Come, I'll show you," she said.

They followed her to the kitchen. Alix unwrapped a paper towel. In it was a half-eaten hot dog, covered with pieces of grass.

"See? I found this right where Maddie was standing. And I was gone for only half a minute. She didn't have *time* to wander away. Somebody gave Maddie this to eat while they caught hold of her."

Mr. Shelby examined the hot dog. "It's still fresh," he said, "so it wasn't there very long." He glanced at his wife. "It does seem suspicious. I'm calling Mr. Tavolott."

"You don't have a phone," Beka reminded him, perching on a step.

"You don't have a phone," Alix said.

"Ah, right."

"Shouldn't you call the *police?*" the girl asked.

"Obviously I can't call *anyone* right now. And I've already walked to Juniper and back once tonight, so it will have to wait until morning."

"Morning?" echoed Alix and the twins.

"Honey, the police won't do anything about a pet who's been missing only a few hours," Mrs. Shelby told her.

"The police won't do anything about a missing pet at all," her husband added. "That's why we should call Mr. Tavolott. He keeps an eye on his resort; he needs to know if dogs are disappearing."

"He's also the mayor of Juniper," Alix told them, as if that would somehow make a difference. She sniffled, trying not to cry.

"Why don't you meet me at Mr. Tavolott's office in the morning?" Mr. Shelby suggested. "Then we can tell him the whole story."

Alix agreed.

"I hear a car," Mrs. Shelby said.

27

"It's probably my dad, coming to get me."

They walked Alix down the drive to her father's car, assuring her they didn't blame her for the dog's disappearance.

The twins trudged to the attic.

Part of Robbie couldn't wait until morning to start looking for the dog thief. And part of him felt guilty over Thatch's being outdoors all night. He *never* ran off without them. . . .

Robbie even felt guilty about Maddie — although there was no way he could have known in advance about the dognapper.

Beka climbed the short ladder to her bunk. "I know you're thinking about Thatch," she said. "He'll be all right, wherever he is. He can take care of himself."

As much as he hated to admit it, Robbie knew his sister was right.

He gazed out the attic window at the moon-dappled forest stretching beyond the backyard. "I know Thatch will be fine on his own," Robbie said. "It's *Maddie* I'm worried about."

6
Ghost Posse

The cloudless morning sky promised a summer-hot day, even though summer hadn't quite made it to Kickingbird — according to the calendar.

Robbie and Beka hurried along the bike path bordering Buffalo Avenue, the main road running through Juniper.

They were tailing Mr. Shelby, who was on his way to meet Alix at Mr. Tavolott's office to discuss the strange disappearance of Maddie and Shawnee.

The air was filled with singing birds, happy to return to the high country after a long winter south.

Yet, in spite of all the cheeriness in the air,

Robbie walked with his head bowed. Thatch hadn't come home last night.

Was he all right?

Yes, Robbie's mind told him. *He's fine; he's a ghost, remember?*

Still, Robbie felt as though Thatch had been dognapped along with Maddie and Shawnee. He was gone, too, wasn't he?

Something else worried Robbie just as much. Last night, Thatch had been suffering from a loss of energy. If Maddie's trail hadn't led him closer to Kickingbird Lake, Robbie knew the dog might be in *real* danger.

The twins weren't sure what happened if they stayed away from the lake too long. Beka had *almost* found out once when she'd *smooshed* into the woodshed and nearly didn't have enough energy to *smoosh* out again.

Robbie remembered how she'd looked — or rather — how she *didn't* look when he'd found her. Her hazy form had almost disappeared.

A chill shivered through him as he remembered. Nothing had scared him *that* much since they'd waded out of the lake all those years ago and discovered no one could see or hear them.

"How can you look so glum on such a pretty morning?" Beka asked. She was practically skipping along the path.

His sister loved summertime, her favorite season. He preferred winter. For twins, they agreed on most things — except this one.

"I'm worried about — "

"Thatch," she finished for him.

"I hate it when you finish my — "

"Sentences."

That did it. Robbie took off after her, chasing his sister down the path, all the way into Juniper.

They bypassed Mr. Shelby, but it was okay. The twins knew how to find Mr. Tavolott's office.

By the time Robbie caught his twin and gave her a good tickling, they were smack in the middle of the bustling town.

The chase had lightened his mood. As a matter of fact, now he was *itching* to do something — like find the mystery boy and his canine captives.

The twins stopped outside an important-looking building marked CITY HALL. Inside, the air was as cool as the marble tile.

They rode the escalator to the second floor. (The twins loved riding the escalator so much, sometimes they came here just to go up and down it for fun.)

At the reception desk sat Miss June, Mr. Tavolott's secretary. She reminded Robbie of his second-grade teacher, with her beehive hairdo and bifocal glasses worn around her neck on a silver chain.

"Good morning, Miss June; we're here to see the mayor," Beka announced.

Miss June kept typing.

"Go right in; he's expecting you," answered Robbie in his best imitation of the secretary's voice.

Beka giggled at his impersonation.

The door was open so they barged in.

Alix was already there, sitting on Mr. Tavolott's sofa while he perched backward in a chair, listening to her story.

The mayor was a large man, usually decked out in a western shirt, cowboy boots, and a black hat.

The twins liked him. He was friendly and kind to all his renters, doing little extras for them, like sending over firewood on snowy nights, or lending phones whenever one was needed.

(Robbie was fascinated by the small phones people carried with them nowadays. He wished they'd been around fifty years ago.)

Alix had just finished giving Mr. Tavolott a detailed account of the last time she saw Shawnee, and was starting her story about Maddie, when Miss June announced the arrival of Mr. Shelby.

He joined Alix on the sofa, listening to her story once more.

"Sounds like both dogs disappeared the same way," Beka said, sitting in a spot of sun on an area rug. "From their own backyards."

Robbie considered the details. "For a dog to be lured away fast, food must be involved."

"June!" called Mr. Tavolott after hearing all the evidence.

The secretary poked her head into the room. Pencils were stuck behind both ears, making her look like an alien from outer space.

"Take a memo," he said.

Miss June rushed back to her desk and returned with a notepad.

"Cancel my afternoon appointments," the mayor began. "I will personally tour the resort to see if anything seems amiss. Next — "

"Wait," Miss June blurted. "I don't have anything to write with." She shuffled through papers on the mayor's desk. "I can never find a pencil when I need one."

Alix was trying her best not to laugh. Mr. Shelby picked up a magazine and pretended to read. Mr. Tavolott simply groaned.

The twins *could* laugh without being heard — so they did.

"Go ahead," Miss June said, holding a borrowed pencil. "I'm ready."

Mr. Tavolott cleared his throat, and continued.

"Holler at Blaze and see if she's heard anything. The locals gather at her diner to talk, so she usually knows the news before Jake does."

The mayor turned to his visitors. "Jake's the editor of the *Juniper Daily News*. Get him on the phone, June, straightaway. I'll ask him to mention the disappearing dogs in his column, so we can nip this dognapping business in the bud."

Miss June dashed off to her tasks.

"Well," finished Mr. Tavolott, "thanks for coming by. We'll round up a posse, so to speak, and do our best to find Maddie and Shawnee. Right now, the only thing you two can do is wait."

They said good-byes and went their separate ways.

The twins followed Alix outside.

Standing on the sidewalk, she squinted into the bright sun, as if trying to determine the time. "I don't *want* to wait," she announced to no one in particular.

"Me neither," Robbie told her.

"*I'm* responsible for Maddie's disappearance, so *I'm* going to find her."

"Attagirl," Beka said.

Alix turned up a side street toward the homes in the hills above Juniper. "I'll round up my *own* posse. Luka will help me."

"Can we join?" Robbie asked. "We have information you need."

"Plus," Beka added, "we have an invisible spy already on the case."

"Which makes the three of us," Robbie finished with a bow, "a ghost posse — at your service."

7

The First Clue

Along the way, Alix stopped at several backyards to talk to the dogs who lived there.

"Hey, Nikki," she called to a black lab behind
a house on Marston Street. "I'm glad you're safe."
She leaned over the fence to rub his nose. "Do *not*
follow any strangers."

On Richmond, Alix stopped to visit Cerise, a
white French poodle. On Kingston, she chatted
with Leo, a bull terrier.

"Must be her clients," Robbie said.

Beka made a goofy face. "Either that, or this
girl is in real need of human friends."

"Be nice." Robbie nudged her. "She's just making sure none of the other dogs in her care are
missing."

At a two-story brick home on Carfax, Alix opened the gate. A golden retriever sprinted around the house to greet her.

"Luka!" Alix exclaimed, kneeling to talk to the dog. "We've got to find Shawnee. Do you understand?"

The dog whined, as though ready to take off on the noble quest.

Alix dashed to the front door, hollering to someone inside that she was taking Luka for a hike to the lake, and would be gone a long time.

Then they were off — the posse of one kid, one dog, and two ghosts.

"Having Thatch's help would make this a whole lot easier," Beka grumbled.

"He *may* be helping," Robbie pointed out. "We just don't know it yet."

Alix and Luka headed north, taking a meandering path which cut through the rolling hills on the outskirts of Juniper, and stopped at the marina, on the south end of Kickingbird Lake.

Coming out of the underbrush and catching a first glimpse of the lake always caught Robbie by surprise. Especially this time of year when trees and bushes were budding back to life.

The color of the water changed constantly. Robbie always suspected that the lake's moods could be read by its hues.

Today, the water reflected the blueness of the sky. Waves crested into snowy foam as a breeze kicked up.

Past the boat launch, the group turned northwest, following the path around the lake.

"We've got to get away from the tourists," Alix told Luka. "If *I* were a dognapper, I'd hide my hostages far from people, in a place where I could visit, but no one could hear them barking."

She stopped on the path, picked up a rock and skipped it across the water. "Too bad Kickingbird is so huge. There must be a zillion hiding places. Where are we going to start?"

Luka was having a grand time, chasing butterflies and barking at sailboats in the distance. But she wasn't doing much to help their quest.

The group circled part of the lake, then hiked into the foothills north of Alpine Lodge, away from the bustling resort.

The path ended, but Alix kept on, winding her way through the forest.

Suddenly Luka stopped. The fur on her neck lifted.

Alix instantly retreated. "Might be a wild animal," she whispered. "Let's go back and try another route."

Luka was happy to obey.

"What is it?" Beka asked.

Robbie stepped cautiously around a tall pine to investigate. He knew ghosts were safe from wild animals. Still, the thought of coming face-to-face with a bear or mountain lion made him uneasy.

A lot of things could have spooked Luka. Maybe the danger she'd sensed had something to do with the mystery boy. Was he near?

"Let's keep going," Robbie suggested.

"But we'll lose Alix." Beka was keeping an eye on the girl, who'd already reached the bottom of the hill where the path had ended.

"It's okay." Robbie climbed around a cluster of boulders. "Alix doesn't know where she's going. We can move faster without her."

"Oh, I get it." Beka hustled to catch up. "You want to find the dogs first, then try to lead Alix to them, right?"

"Sounds like a good plan to me."

"But — "

A rustling in the huckleberry bushes stopped her before she could finish.

"Must be the animal who scared Luka," Robbie said. "Maybe it's hurt." He moved toward the sound.

"Careful, Raz," Beka warned.

Robbie moved slowly through the tall grass, ready to bolt if something leaped out in front of him.

A whine made him freeze. It sounded familiar. "Thatch?" he whispered. "Is that you?"

The answering cry led him to the base of a budding sassafras tree.

"Puppy!" Beka rushed to kneel next to Thatch.

He was stretched out on his stomach, pulling himself forward a little at a time. And he was pale — more see-through than usual.

"Do you think he's sick? Injured? Or do you think that . . . that dognapper did something to him?" Beka's voice rose with every word.

"Raz, he's a ghost," Robbie reminded her. "He's not sick or injured, and nobody did anything to him."

"Then what — ?"

Thatch's forlorn expression almost broke Robbie's heart. "I'll bet he's trying to make it to the lake. He stayed up all night, remember? After wearing himself out playing with Maddie."

"We've got to help him." Beka boosted Thatch's rump. Robbie lifted his front end, then led the way, cutting across the hill straight toward the lake, trying to keep his balance on the uneven ground.

The nearer they drew to the water, the more

Thatch perked up. By the time they'd made it to the lake path, he started wriggling to get down.

In minutes he began to trot, then he took off like a rock from a slingshot, tearing all the way to shore, and splashing in the water.

Robbie knew how the dog felt. He experienced the same burst of energy whenever he neared the lake.

That, alone, never ceased to amaze him, yet what astonished him more, was that Thatch *knew* he needed to return to the lake.

"You're one smart dog," Robbie called, watching him act like his old self again.

"No kidding," Beka agreed. "He just gave us our first clue."

"He did?" Robbie's mind replayed the last twenty minutes. *What did I miss?*

Beka grinned, as though daring him to read her mind.

Sometimes he could; sometimes he couldn't. Shrugging, he gave up.

Casually, she pointed in the direction where they'd rescued Thatch. "*That's* the way to the dognapper's den."

A lightbulb clicked on in Robbie's brain. Of course. Thatch must have been making a beeline from the boy's hideout to the lake.

"Good deduction, Sherlock," he said. "You're *almost* as smart as my favorite dog."

He didn't hear Beka's answer.

He was too busy dashing toward the water to chase his *favorite dog* along the rocky shore of Kickingbird Lake.

8
The Mystery Boy

Robbie hopped onto a boulder jutting out between a grove of junipers. His eyes searched for a familiar landmark.

Where were they? This was a part of Moosehead National Forest he'd never explored. The only signs of civilization they had passed were cross-country ski trails, and an occasional sign marking the way for skiers and hikers.

"I think we're due north of the lodge," Beka offered. "But we've never come this far before."

Robbie shaded his eyes. "I can see one of the ski slopes on Walrus Mountain."

"Where?" Beka climbed onto the rock to look. "We need to know where we are or we won't know where we find what we're looking for."

"Huh?" Robbie laughed. "Say that again in English?"

"I *mean*," she began.

"I know what you mean. But if we get lost, we can follow one of the ski trails. They all end up at the lodge — eventually."

Robbie leaped off the boulder to appease Thatch, who was dashing up the rocky hill, then back again, eager for them to follow. "At least we know we're heading in the right direction. Our ghost guide knows exactly where we're going."

"Thatch makes a much better leader than Alix," Beka agreed. "But I wish I knew what he's leading us into."

"Only one way to find out." Robbie motioned for her to follow.

The twins continued to the top of the rocky rise, then started down into a lush valley. Below, a stream sliced a narrow meadow in half. Beyond the far bank was a dense forest.

Any other day, the woods would have beckoned invitingly to Robbie. But today, the shadowed trees looked foreboding. Were they sheltering the boy who'd dognapped Shawnee and Maddie?

"We're close," Robbie said.

"How do you know?" Beka grabbed Thatch to hold him until they found a good place to scale down the grassy slope.

"Listen."

Above the birdcalls and the trickling stream came a muffled bark. Then another.

Thatch gave an answering, *"Woof."*

"They can't hear you," Beka teased, patting his head.

Robbie wondered whether or not her remark was true. Hadn't Maddie seen Thatch? Maybe she could *hear* him as well.

"Get ready," Beka warned.

She let go of the dog's collar. He charged down the hill.

The twins took off after him.

In one smooth leap, Thatch cleared the stream and disappeared into the trees.

Robbie turned on the speed, jumping over rocks and sidestepping mountain cactuses bursting with yellow flowers.

When he got to the stream, he copied Thatch, sailing over it, higher and farther than humanly possible.

Beka chose to splash into the rushing water and wade across. When she climbed the far bank, her clothes were completely dry.

Being a ghost had its perks.

"Which way did Thatch go?" Beka blinked, letting her eyes adjust to the shade in the woods.

45

"Thatch!" Robbie called, hoping the dog wouldn't leave them behind.

In a few seconds, he appeared, gazing at them as if saying, *"Come on. You guys are too slow."*

They wound their way up the hill through dense trees, hustling to keep up with their four-footed leader.

A ski trail cut through the forest. Thatch turned onto the pathway, going faster.

After a few more twists and turns, they came to a warming hut. The huts were used by cross-country skiers, giving them a place to rest, get warm, or eat a snack.

The twins came to an abrupt stop.

Beyond the hut, in a clearing, was a boy. The same boy who'd been snooping around the backyard of the Zuffel house last night. The mystery boy. The dognapper.

Chained to a stake in the ground were two dogs. Maddie and another, who looked just like Luka, which meant it had to be Shawnee.

"Is he the same boy you saw last night?" Beka whispered.

"Yes." Robbie glanced at her. "Why are you whispering?"

"I don't want him to hear me." She bit her lip. "Whoops. Sometimes I forget I'm a ghost."

With that, Beka shouted "HEY! WHAT ARE YOU DOING?" at the top of her lungs. She raced right up to the boy, planting fists on both her hips, as though she demanded an immediate explanation.

The boy reacted. Twirling in place, he scanned his surroundings, a panicked look on his face. Then he began to shiver, even though the early afternoon sun had warmed the forest to T-shirt temperature.

People always reacted — one way or another — whenever they'd been chilled by a ghost twin.

With a happy *yip*, Maddie raced to meet Thatch — as far as her chain would take her. They rubbed noses in greeting.

Shawnee didn't seem to notice the ghost dog, but she *did* stand at attention — proving she *sensed* something weird was happening.

"Mmm," Robbie said. "If Maddie can see Thatch, why can't Shawnee?" Sometimes ghost rules weren't logical. *But then*, he reminded himself, *being a ghost isn't logical, either*.

Robbie studied the scene. He and the boy were the exact same height, even had the same wavy brown hair.

Somehow, Robbie expected the dognapper to

be a mean, evil-looking person, but here was a boy who looked enough like him to be his brother — minus the glasses.

And he wasn't mean at all. He was petting Shawnee, talking to her in a soothing voice. Then he moved across the clearing. "Shawnee," he called in a firm tone.

"He knows their names," Beka said.

"That's because he watched them with their owners before he dognapped them," Robbie reminded her.

"Come!" the boy ordered.

Shawnee ducked her head, as if unsure at first, then trotted toward the boy. Her chain was longer than Robbie had thought. It allowed her to move at least twenty yards. The boy must have attached a whole lot of leashes together to make the chains that lengthy.

At least it made Robbie feel better. He hadn't liked seeing the dogs chained at all. The next sight pleased him, too. The boy rewarded Shawnee with food.

"He's training them," Beka said.

"And he's feeding them." Robbie moved closer for a better look. "Pieces of hot dogs," he added.

Robbie had feared they might find the dogs

abandoned and hungry, but the dognapper *did* have a conscience after all.

"Maddie!" the boy snapped in a voice that meant business.

Maddie left Thatch's side, responding to the call, standing at attention.

"Food wins over puppy love," Beka noted wryly.

"Come," the boy commanded.

Maddie bounded to the boy, and duly received her treat.

Thatch wanted a treat, too. He darted after Maddie. She snipped at him before grabbing her share of the hot dog from the boy's hand.

Thatch didn't like being left out. He watched the boy, circling, as though trying to second-guess him.

"Uh-oh," Beka said. "Not sharing treats with a ghost dog isn't a wise move."

She glanced at Robbie. "Well? Have you figured all this out yet? Why did the boy kidnap the dogs? Just to *train* them? It doesn't make sense."

"Let's watch and see if we can find out." Robbie settled onto a flat rock. Beka joined him.

The boy worked the dogs one at a time, teaching them basic commands: *Come. Heel. Whoa. Fetch.*

What the dogs fetched was a large glove, filled with sticks or rocks to make it heavy. Only the boy didn't call it a *glove*; he called it a *bird*.

Every time the dogs responded correctly, they were rewarded.

Thatch was getting more and more agitated at being left out of all the fun — and treats.

Finally he'd had enough. The next time the boy produced a slice of hot dog to reward Maddie, Thatch raced ahead of her, and snapped it right out of the boy's hand.

Robbie chuckled. He'd seen Thatch do this before.

The dog's natural intensity made it easy for him. The *twins*, however, had to concentrate like crazy to make something in "this world" move.

Robbie waited to see the boy's shocked reaction at the disappearing hot dog. But the reaction was *not* what he expected.

The boy snarled, "*You* again. Go home. I don't need you."

Robbie came to his feet. "Raz! He can *see* Thatch!"

"How did Thatch *do* that?"

"I don't know. But it sounds as though the guy's seen Thatch before."

"Are you thinking what I'm thinking?" The

wicked grin spreading across Beka's face matched the thoughts tumbling through Robbie's mind.

"We can try," he said. "If Thatch has cracked open the window from our world to his world . . ." Robbie paused to return her wicked grin. "Let's see if we can shove that window open all the way. . . ."

9

A New Rule

The twins moved across the "training area," stationing themselves on each side of Thatch.

"Think VISIBLE," Beka said, then shot her brother a sheepish look. "I'm just guessing, of course."

"Learn from Thatch," Robbie suggested. "When the boy ignored him, he wanted to be seen so badly, it made him visible. We need to think the same way."

The twins fell silent, willing their bodies to obey their thoughts.

The boy continued putting the dogs through their paces.

Every few moments, he'd glare at Thatch, saying, "Go home and don't come back. If anyone follows you here, they'll find me. All I need is another day or two. Then I'll be finished with the dogs."

The boy's words broke Robbie's concentration. *Finished with the dogs? Then what?* The possibilities weren't ones Robbie wanted to consider.

Beka nudged him, as if she knew his thoughts were straying.

He renewed his efforts, squinting at the boy. Think *solid. Concrete. Dense.* Think *shape* and *form* and *wholeness.*

A sensation rippled from his head to his toes. He'd never felt it before. It was a sudden heaviness, like Thatch had just hopped on top of him.

Only the dog was still by his side, watching and whimpering, bound to obey the boy's command to stay away, yet wanting to be part of the fun.

Beside him, Beka shifted, as if she'd felt a weight coming down on her, too, and was trying to steady herself.

Suddenly Robbie recognized the heaviness. He hadn't felt it for fifty years. Not since he was a solid human being.

The boy started to snap at Thatch once more, then stopped. His jaw fell open as he gaped in their direction.

"Who . . . who?" he babbled, then stumbled toward the stake and unhooked the chains.

"Yeah!" Robbie cheered. "He's letting the dogs go!"

No such luck. The boy yanked the dogs back to the warming hut.

Beka chased after him. "Hey, you!" she hollered. "Stop!"

Robbie was just about to remind her that the action was pointless, when the boy shrank away from her.

"He can *see* you!" Robbie yelped, scrambling to catch up.

The boy forced the dogs inside the hut. Unhooking their chains, he tossed them onto the floor, jerked the door shut, and padlocked it.

With one terrified glance at the twins, he bolted down the trail.

"It worked!" Robbie danced across the clearing, even though he was disappointed. He'd *hoped* the boy would drop the chains and run, leaving the dogs free to dash home.

Beka grasped Thatch's front paws to join the dancing. "We've discovered a new ghost rule!" she sang. "A new power we didn't know we had — thanks to our puppy ghost teacher."

Thatch didn't much care for dancing. Pulling away, he trotted back to the hut, leaving Beka to dance by herself.

Robbie examined the training area. "I'm sure he *saw* us, but I don't think he *heard* us."

"We didn't say much," Beka reminded him, ending her dance with a fairy twirl. "So, what are we waiting for? Let's follow the dognapper home and find out who he is."

"Only if Thatch comes with us." Robbie didn't want to take off again without their dog.

The twins called him. They begged. They teased.

The ghost dog would *not* budge from his job of standing guard.

"Ah, true love," Beka moaned. "At least now we know where he is."

She tugged Robbie's sleeve. "Let's *go* or we'll lose the boy."

Giving one last pat to Thatch, Robbie reluctantly hurried after Beka.

Catching up with the dognapper was easy.

Fear — or running — had taken away his breath. By the time he reached the far side of the valley, he'd slowed to a nervous walk, throwing worried glances over one shoulder.

"Hey!" Beka hollered. "Can you still see us?"

He seemed to be looking *through* them, not *at* them.

"Guess not," Robbie said. The heaviness in

his body was gone now. He felt light on his feet again.

The twins fell into line behind the boy.

"Making ourselves visible was hard," Beka said. "Did you feel your energy draining?"

"Yes, but maybe it'll get easier. Remember how hard it was to *smoosh* the first few times? Now we can do it faster — except I still end up with a headache."

"Well, *getting solid* practically killed me."

Robbie laughed at her poor choice of words. He watched her dodge a quick sparrow who almost zoomed through her stomach.

"I wonder how we *looked* to him?" she mused. "Like ourselves? Or like some storybook ghosts?"

"We looked scary, or he wouldn't have panicked and run. But hey," Robbie added, grinning, "it's our *job* to be scary."

The boy led them beyond Juniper to the far edge of town, almost to the turnoff for the main highway.

It was a long walk. Finally, he headed down an alley, then hopped over a back fence.

The ghost duo followed, circling to the front of the house. On the mailbox was the name TILLER.

Robbie glanced up and down the street to get his bearings, in case he had to find the house again.

"Carson, is that you?" called a voice as soon as the boy (and twins) went inside.

The boy mumbled an answer, then hurried to a bedroom. The room was packed with kids — a half dozen girls, all about seven or eight years old.

"Crimeny," Robbie exclaimed. "Do all these kids *live* here?"

Beka shrugged. "I count four beds; maybe they do."

"Can't you and your friends play somewhere else?" the boy — Carson — grumbled. "This is the *boys'* room, lest you forget."

"The boys' room?" Beka echoed.

"Cindy's club is meeting in our room," one of the girls answered.

Disgusted, the boy grabbed a book and headed through the house.

Sounds of kids shouting and babies crying made Robbie appreciate the quiet Zuffel house, yet he wondered what it'd be like to have a whole bunch of brothers and sisters.

"*How to Train Hunting Dogs*," Beka said.

"Huh?"

"That's the name of the book he's carrying."

"Good observation, Sherlock."

Carson stopped in the dining room, disappearing under a tablecloth that touched the floor on all sides.

"No need to follow *him* anymore," Robbie muttered.

As he started to wonder how they were going to get out of the house, a woman appeared. A harried-looking woman, carrying a baby on one hip.

"Carson, are you in your office?" she teased.

"Mmm-mm," the boy answered, sounding as though he didn't think her joke was funny.

"Why is it so cold in this room?" she asked. "It's hot outside."

"Sorry," Beka said. "Free air-conditioning. No charge."

"We'll be leaving now if you'll kindly open the screen door," Robbie told her.

When the woman received no answer from her son, she disappeared down the hall.

"How rude," Beka said. "You asked her to open the door and she ignored you."

"Should be easy to get out." Robbie stationed himself in front of the screen. "Get ready to *smoosh*," he said.

Beka stood beside him. They concentrated, eyes closed, picturing themselves on the other side of the door.

In seconds, Robbie's skin started to tingle. An airplane roared overhead — or was it *inside* his head?

Dizziness pulled the rug out from under his feet. He began to fall.

10

The Search Is On

But Robbie wasn't falling.

He was *smooshing.*

Smooshing through the tiny holes in the screen.

Opening his eyes, he found himself sprawled on the front porch. Beka was beside him.

A headache throbbed his temples, making him feel as if he was sitting inside a clanging church bell.

While Robbie recovered, Beka pulled herself to her feet. She always snapped out of the after-effects of *smooshing* much faster than he did.

On the way home, the twins discussed the possible meaning of Carson's words: *All I need is a day or two. Then I'll be finished with the dogs.*

Beka looked worried. "You don't think he'd get

rid of the dogs, do you? I mean, how . . . ?" Her voice trailed off.

Robbie thought about the warming hut. "All Carson would have to do is close the air vents, remove the lock, and take out the food and water. Make it look like the dogs wandered into the hut, the door blew shut, and . . ." He couldn't put it into words, either.

"He wouldn't," Beka said.

Robbie gave her a somber look. "Who knows what a desperate dognapper might do? Especially if he knows *ghosts* are hot on his trail. . . ."

Near the house, the twins caught up with the Shelbys, walking home from their three-hour boat tour of Kickingbird Lake.

Robbie and Beka listened to them discuss the sights they'd seen: the ghost town near Ragged River, Danger Cove, Mystery Island.

Beep! Beep!

Everyone's attention was drawn toward the road.

Mr. Tavolott's jeep zipped past them and turned up the curved drive in front of the Zuffel house.

When the jeep stopped, Alix hopped out, holding the door while a golden retriever jumped to the ground.

Robbie's heart leaped when he saw the dog —

Carson had been caught! The dogs had been freed!

But it wasn't Shawnee. . . .

"This is Luka," Alix called to the Shelbys, then waited while they hurried up the drive. "She looks just like her sister."

"And Thatch looks just like Maddie," Robbie mumbled.

He listened to his own words, replaying them inside his head: *Shawnee and Luka. Look-alike dogs. Carson took one and left the other.*

Thatch and Maddie. Two more look-alike dogs.

Carson had seen Thatch at the warming hut. Had he also seen Thatch in the backyard, playing with Maddie? Had Carson thought he was taking one dog and leaving the other?

A dognapper with heart, Robbie scoffed. *He wanted the dogs, yet he wanted the owners to have a pet, too. Mmm.*

The group stayed on the veranda to talk. Luka had the run of the front yard. The honeymooners sat on a wooden bench saved from the old train station in Juniper before it was torn down.

"Any news?" Mr. Shelby asked.

Mr. Tavolott leaned against the porch railing. "The police are on alert. Tomorrow's newspapers will warn residents to keep an eye on their pets, and a group of park rangers are combing the forests around the lake."

"That's a good start," said Mrs. Shelby.

"Why doesn't Mr. Tavolott's news make Alix look any happier?" Beka asked.

Robbie glanced at the girl. She was watching Luka with a forlorn look on her face. "Doesn't make *me* happy, either. Mr. Tavolott's *posse* is searching the wrong area. Carson and the dogs are nowhere near the lake."

"By the time they figure it out," Beka added, "it might be too late."

Robbie gave her a reluctant nod.

"What else can we do?" Alix asked in a quiet voice.

No one answered, which made Robbie feel worse.

"Oh, Alix, we got you something." Mrs. Shelby shuffled through the bags of souvenirs they'd carried home. "Here."

Alix ran up the veranda steps and took the gift. Opening a small box, she pulled out a wood carving of a golden retriever. Her eyes lit up, then she looked sad again.

"Thank you," she mumbled. "I'm going to carry it with me until I find Shawnee."

Mr. Tavolott donned his cowboy hat, and headed toward the jeep. "I'll keep ya'll posted." He waved good-bye. "Alix? Can I give you a lift to town?"

"No thanks," she answered, shoving the wooden dog into her pocket. "I'll walk Luka home."

Mr. Tavolott glanced at the darkening sky. "Get going soon," he warned her. "And be careful. Hold tight to Luka's leash."

After promises and good-byes, Beka started into the house with the Shelbys.

"Wait," Robbie called.

Beka gave him a questioning look. "Either we go in while the door's open or we're stuck outside," she reminded him.

"I think we should follow Alix," he said. "Just in case she decides to go looking for Shawnee instead of going home."

"But it's getting dark."

"That's why we need to follow her."

"I've walked a zillion miles today," Beka grumbled. "All I want is to curl up on my bunk with one of my library books."

"And with Thatch, too?"

She gave him the same forlorn look Alix had been wearing.

"Good point. How can I relax without my puppy?" She glanced longingly toward the door, watching it slam shut for the night. "Okay, let's go. The sooner we get this over with, the sooner Thatch will come back."

The twins followed Alix down Deer Creek to the fork, where Aspen shoots north to the national park, and Buffalo runs east into Juniper.

Alix paused at the crossroads. She let go of Luka's leash while she gazed north, and studied the sky.

"She's trying to decide if she has time to snoop around Moosehead before it gets too dark," Robbie said.

"Go home, go home, go home," Beka chanted. "We'll help you tomorrow. We promise."

Alix still hesitated. Pulling the wooden dog from her pocket, she rubbed it, as she would a magic lantern offering three wishes.

"Go home," Beka repeated. "We know where Shawnee is, and we'll take you to her tomorrow — if you'll let us."

Alix trudged in a slow circle, deciding what to do. Darkness was claiming the valley faster than normal because of an overcast sky.

Clicking her tongue at Luka, she returned the wooden dog to her pocket, and started off toward Juniper.

"Yea!" cheered Beka. "She listened to me."

"Here, girl!"

The twins stopped.

"Who said that?" Robbie turned in a circle, searching for the source of the voice.

Behind the border of shrubs which lined the path came another muffled call.

Luka froze, ears lifted.

Alix froze, too, then lunged to snatch the dog's leash and wrap a protective arm around her.

The bushes parted.

A figure stepped onto the path.

Robbie waited for his eyes to adjust in the dim light.

Beside him, Beka gave a little gasp.

It was Carson, slithering from the shadows, bending over Luka to pet her. "Nice dog you've got here," he said to Alix. "Isn't this the one you call Luka?"

11

Phantom Escorts

Alix kept a firm grip on Luka's leash. "Who are you and how did you know my dog's name?"

Carson hesitated before answering, which made Robbie assume he was trying to come up with a good excuse.

"Um, well we go to the same school. I've seen you at Hanover."

"You're not in my class," Alix answered, giving him a suspicious glare.

"I didn't say I was; I said I've *seen* you at school."

"So, how'd you know Luka's name?"

He began to fuss over the dog, as if trying to avoid the question.

Robbie didn't miss the fact that Luka was sniffing Carson's hands like crazy. Did they carry the recent scent of Shawnee?

The boy cleared his throat. "I must have heard you talking about your dogs — in the hallway at school, or on the playground."

"*Dogs?*" Clutching the leash, Alix backed away. "I didn't mention another dog. Why'd you say *dogs?*"

"Attagirl," Beka growled. "Go get him."

"Yeah," Robbie added. "Ask him how he knew this wasn't Shawnee."

Carson pulled off his glasses, fumbling to clean them with his shirt. "I — I meant to say *dog;* it was a mistake. I just . . . I like dogs."

"Do you have one?"

Robbie loved the way Alix was giving the guy the third degree.

"Huh? Oh, well, I'd *like* to have a dog. I'm trying to talk my father into it. But I have five sisters and three brothers, so my parents don't think we have room for a pet."

"Wow," Alix said, softening a little. "I don't have *any* brothers and sisters."

"But you've got do — um, you've got a dog."

"He's acting so *guilty*," Beka snipped. "Can't she see through him?"

"Not as much as I can see through *you*," Robbie teased.

Beka groaned at his joke. "And I, you," she countered.

Alix relaxed her hold on Luka's chain — but only a little. "Doesn't your father *like* dogs?"

"Sure." Carson's eyes lit up. "He even hunts with bird dogs. Quail, pheasant, and grouse. Only he uses his friends' trained hunting dogs." The light in his eyes faded.

Robbie exchanged glances with his sister.

"Trained hunting dogs?" Beka repeated. "Isn't that what Carson was doing with Maddie and Shawnee? Training them?"

Robbie's brain was trying to sort out all the clues he was hearing. "But why? He can't show up at home with two trained dogs. Won't his dad question where they came from?"

"I'd hope so."

Beka was practically standing on top of Carson — just to make him uneasy. "Besides," she added, "as soon as Carson unhooked the dogs' leashes, they'd probably dash straight for home."

"Shawnee would," Robbie agreed. "But Maddie wouldn't know where home was."

Alix lifted her chin. "I have a dog-sitting business," she bragged.

"You do?" Carson's eyebrows rose above his glasses.

"Some of my clients are park rangers in Moosehead, and some live in Juniper. I even dog-sit for tourists."

Alix's expression changed, as though she suddenly recalled what had happened last time she dog-sat for tourists — the Shelbys.

"That's so cool." Carson kicked at the gravel on the road. "Do you, um, ever need help? Taking care of the dogs?"

Alix shrugged. "If more than one person needs me at the same time, I take all the dogs together."

"Will you tell me if I can help you sometime?" The look in Carson's eyes was one of hope. "I live in the last house on Knox Drive."

Alix acted as if she wasn't sure about taking an offer from someone who'd come leaping out of the bushes at her. Someone who already knew her dog's name.

"Oh," he added. "I'm Carson Tiller."

A look of recognition spilled onto her face. "I'm Alix Silver. Do you have a sister named Leigh Tiller?"

He nodded.

"She's in my class."

"My sisters and brothers are in *every* class at Hanover."

Alix laughed, then glanced at the orange sunset. "I've got to get home."

"Fine. I'm going this way, too."

They took off, walking side by side, the dog scampering along between them.

Carson rested one hand on Luka's head as he walked.

Robbie hoped it wasn't a sign that he was claiming possession.

"We don't need to follow them any farther, do we?" Beka crinkled her face at Robbie. "It's been a long day, and I have a funny feeling tomorrow's going to be even longer."

Robbie was torn. "But what if Carson tries to get the dog away from her? Shouldn't we escort Alix all the way, just in case?" He didn't trust Carson, not after what the boy had done.

"I guess you're right." Beka's frown changed into a mischievous grin. "Let's give Alix a *phantom escort*. And if Carson tries anything funny, we'll make another *personal appearance* before he can get away. . . ."

12

Do the Ghost Float

Robbie stretched out on the bench inside the octagon-shaped gazebo. His sister lounged on the swing in the middle.

The twins had decided to spend the night outside instead of *smooshing* into the house.

When they lived here as "real kids," they couldn't wait for their first backyard camp-out. As soon as winter stepped aside and let spring warm the nights, they'd be out here in the gazebo.

Back then, however, they'd come with pillows, blankets, snacks, and flashlights to beam onto comic book pages.

And Thatch, to stand guard. Only he was always first to fall asleep.

Robbie'd never heard a dog snore as loudly as

Thatch. He could scare away burglars with his *snore* instead of his *bark*.

Don't think about Thatch, his mind told him. *He's fine. And his mission is a noble one.*

The slight breeze ruffled Robbie's hair as he clasped his hands behind his head and gazed at the stars, now peeking through dark holes where clouds had disappeared.

Carson had been a perfect gentleman tonight. He hadn't tried anything underhanded, like snatching Luka's leash and dashing away.

Instead, he walked Alix home, sharing "dog tips" with her:

- Always trim a dog's coat in summer to help him keep cool.
- Puppies can learn their names and simple commands, coming when called, and knowing what "no" means.
- Dog biscuits will keep a dog's teeth clean.

It was at times like those Robbie wished he could reach into *this world* and join conversations. *He* knew a lot about dogs, too.

He remembered the night they found baby Thatch, abandoned in the forest north of Kickingbird Lake. Dr. Vetta told them Thatch was only six weeks old.

The doctor had given them basic dog-training tips, plus a booklet called *How to Train Your Puppy*.

Too bad Robbie couldn't have shared *his* tips. Like:

- Give your dog toys because they trigger his instinct to hunt and capture his food.
- Don't give a large water bowl to a small dog, or a small bowl to a large dog.
- Feed a puppy twice a day, and an older dog once a day.

Oh, well. Alix and Carson probably knew all those things anyway.

Carson. What a puzzle. He seemed like an okay person. Yet, how could he take away a family's pet? Even if he *did* think he was leaving one behind.

The *squeak-squeak* of the gazebo swing told him Beka wasn't calm and relaxed.

"What's the matter?" Robbie asked, sitting up.

Moonlight made his sister's hazy form glow with a buttery brightness.

"Doesn't it bother you that Carson is making

friends with Alix? I mean, he stole her dog. How can he act like her friend?"

"He found someone who likes dogs as much as he does."

Beka shifted, trying to find a comfortable position on the swing. "Well, tomorrow, we'll see how friendly Alix is after she learns the truth."

That's what Robbie was hoping, too. "Only one problem," he said. "How are we going to make Alix *find* the warming hut?"

"You mean, you don't have a plan yet?" Beka teased.

Robbie lay back and closed his eyes. "Not yet. Let's sleep on it and see what we come up with in the morning."

"We haven't slept for fifty years," Beka reminded him.

"You know what I mean." Robbie kicked her swing. "Be quiet, close your eyes, and do the *ghost float*."

13
Witness to a *Smooshing*

In the morning, the twins didn't know whether to strike out for the warming hut, or follow Alix.

Robbie stepped from the gazebo to check the weather — windy, yet warm — unusually warm. He squinted at the cloudless sky. Summer seemed to be arriving early in Kickingbird this year.

"I *really* want to go back to the hut and check on Thatch," Robbie said. "To make sure he's okay."

His sister was trying to finger-comb her hair. Giving up, she let the wind rearrange it. "Well, *I* think we should follow Alix. The best way to help Maddie and Shawnee is by making sure they're found — by a real person."

Robbie was torn.

"Why don't *you* hike up to see Thatch," Beka suggested. "And *I'll* go after Alix."

He considered her idea. "I wish we had two of those mini phones so we could keep in touch." He thought of the "phones" he and Beka once made out of empty soup cans connected with a string. They worked from one end of the yard to the other — but only as far as the string would stretch.

"Fine," Robbie said, agreeing to her plan.

He headed north, while Beka headed east.

When Robbie came to the ranger booth at the archway into Moosehead National Park, he gave a polite wave to the lady ranger on duty as he breezed through.

"Don't need a map," he called. "I know this area as well as I know my own backyard."

The ranger, of course, didn't respond.

Robbie bypassed the hikers' trails, and chose a direct route, cutting across the rolling foothills. He scanned familiar landmarks, trying to determine the quickest way to get to the warming hut.

The route he chose was *not* the easiest way. Whenever he came to a thick growth of prickly bushes, he'd sprint ahead, then take a running leap and sail right over the obstacle.

After a few tries, he'd perfected the *ghost leap*.

It worked well on steep or slippery boulders, too.

"Nifty," Robbie mumbled, pleased to discover this quicker way of traipsing through the forest. For the next half hour, he *ghost-leaped* over everything in his path, eager to share his discovery with Beka.

Thatch wouldn't be impressed. To the ghost dog, it would be old news — something *he'd* discovered long ago.

At the warming hut, Robbie's heart stalled.

Thatch was nowhere in sight.

Neither was Carson — but it was still early.

Doesn't make sense, his mind told him. *If Thatch had a reason to leave, he would have come straight home.*

Unless Carson had *moved* the dogs.

Had the ghosts' appearance scared Carson so badly, he'd found a different hiding place? The thought of spending another long day searching for the dogs did *not* appeal to Robbie.

He sat down by the door of the hut to think.

A slight whimper met his ears. The dogs were still here!

"Maddie!" Robbie called. "Shawnee!"

Barking erupted from the hut. A bark that sounded very familiar.

"Thatch!" Robbie hollered. "Are you in there, too?"

Had his dog rushed into the hut with the other dogs and gotten locked in? He had reasons to go inside — mainly Maddie and food.

Robbie was relieved to find Thatch. Still, he wanted to touch him, pet him. Not a day had gone by without a wriggly hug from his favorite dog.

Stepping back, he took a good look at the warming hut. There were plenty of air vents and knotholes to *smoosh* through. "Here, boy," he called. "Come out so I can see you."

The answering *yip* told Robbie his dog wanted to obey. Thatch's "need for being needed" was almost as great as his need for treats.

Robbie had never observed anyone *smooshing* before. He was usually doing it at the same time. Fascinated, he watched and waited, circling the hut so he wouldn't miss anything.

In seconds, white "steam" began to seep from an air vent.

As Robbie stared, the swirling mass floated to the ground, turning milky and lumpy-looking, becoming larger and more solid by the second.

The mass took on the shape of a dog. At the last instant, the process sped up, as if someone had pushed a *fast-forward* button.

Thatch became Thatch.

He flumped to the ground on his belly, legs out as if he'd started to leap before the *smooshing* took over, then landed before his legs had time to finish the movement.

For a few seconds, the dog seemed dazed.

Robbie grinned, wondering if he was suffering a *smooshing* headache. He massaged Thatch's neck until the dog recovered and leaped to his paws, rewarding Robbie with slobbery kisses and love nips.

With Thatch half in, half out of his lap, Robbie leaned against the hut to wait for Carson.

And, hopefully soon, the arrival of Beka and Alix.

14
The Secrets of Being a Ghost

Finding Alix was easy.

When Beka arrived, the girl was already in her backyard, waiting for Luka to finish breakfast.

After the dog had lapped her last tongueful of water, Alix snapped a leash onto her collar and led Luka out the gate and down the walk.

"Big day," Alix said to the dog. "You and I are going to track down Shawnee."

Luka *woofed* when she heard her sister's name.

"Smart dog," Beka said. "*Almost* as smart as Thatch. But not quite. I'll bet Luka can't leap ten-foot fences, or go outside without waiting for a door to open."

Beka hushed, feeling guilty for bragging. Shawnee and Luka *were* nifty dogs.

Suddenly Alix stopped — so abruptly, Beka stepped *into* her.

Cringing at the eerie feeling, she quickly hopped away.

Alix shuddered, glancing at the sky, as though checking to see if a cold front had suddenly blown into Juniper.

"Sorry," Beka muttered.

Shrugging it off, Alix said. "Luka, should we go get Carson first?"

Beka caught her breath. "NO!" she hollered.

"Carson wanted to help me with the dogs," Alix added. "Maybe he could help me track Shawnee. Especially since you and I didn't do so well yesterday on our own. . . ."

"Bad decision," Beka told her. "Who knows what he might do if he finds out you're on his trail?"

Still, the girl paused.

Beka followed Alix's gaze to see what held her attention.

The street sign. They'd come to Knox Drive. Carson's street.

Beka stepped in front of Alix. "Don't go get him," she insisted. "You don't really *know* him.

And it's more important to find the dogs. Let Mr. Tavolott deal with Carson."

Beka repeated the words several times — just in case.

Alix fidgeted with Luka's chain as she mulled over her decision. "I don't really know him," she muttered. "And something about him bothered me."

"Bothered you *so* much, you didn't even tell him about Shawnee," Beka added. "Am I right?"

"That's why I didn't tell him about Shawnee," Alix echoed.

"So." Beka loved being right. "Go on by yourself. Go on, go on, go on." Chanting words helped them sink into a person's brain, she'd discovered.

And they did.

Changing direction, Alix began to jog down the sidewalk. Luka broke into a trot, matching her pace.

Good news: Alix wasn't heading toward Carson's house.

Bad news: She wasn't heading toward the warming hut, either.

Beka jogged along behind. *How can I convince her to veer northwest? To head toward the foothills north of Alpine Lodge?*

She pondered the problem. As a ghost, she

hadn't had much experience convincing people to do what she *wanted* them to do.

Was there a ghostly way to make Alix hustle in the right direction?

Sometimes Beka wished she'd stumble across a book at the library called *The Secrets of Being a Ghost*.

Ha, she thought, laughing at the idea. *Maybe I should write it!*

15

The Making of a Bird Dog

A rustling in the bushes brought Robbie to his feet.

Carson burst into the clearing, out of breath.

Why was he in such a hurry?

Robbie lunged away from the door of the warming hut to keep Carson from rushing into him.

He didn't miss Thatch's growl as the boy unlocked the door.

Thatch sensed *something* about Carson. Had he been mean to the dogs?

Shawnee and Maddie leaped outside, but not before Carson clipped on their leashes.

Robbie stepped into the hut. The food bowls were empty; the water bowl was half full.

Carson hooked the dogs' chains to the stake in

the clearing, then returned to the hut. With brisk motions, he swept the floor with an old broom, then filled the food and water bowls with supplies kept on a bench.

Robbie was relieved to see the boy taking care of the dogs' needs.

Except dogs also needed fresh air and sunshine and lots of room to exercise.

"One more day," Carson told Maddie and Shawnee. "Let's make it a good one."

One more day until what?

Robbie let Thatch dash about, playing with Maddie, until Carson scolded Maddie for not following his commands.

"Thatch, come here!" Robbie called. "You're getting your girlfriend into trouble." He grasped Thatch's collar, proud that *his* dog knew how to listen and obey commands. "How come Carson could see you yesterday, but he can't today?"

If the ghost dog knew the answer, he didn't share it with Robbie.

Carson went to work, training the dogs. Holding one back, he'd toss the weighted glove across the clearing. "Fetch the bird!" he'd cry.

The dog would tear after the "glove-bird," snatch it up, and trot back, dropping it at Carson's feet. *Most* of the time.

When she didn't, Carson would scold her and

refuse to offer a treat. He'd make her do it over until she got it right — and earned her treats and praises.

Then Carson would switch dogs and start over.

"He's teaching them to fetch birds," Robbie said out loud, doing his best to keep Thatch from dashing after the glove. "Beka was right. He's training them to be hunting dogs."

Robbie's mind stayed on Beka. He hoped she'd found Alix by now.

Turning his attention back to Carson, he tried to recall everything the boy had told Alix. His father hunted birds, but didn't have a dog. "Maybe," Robbie mused, "he's doing this to *prove* to his father that he *can* train a dog."

He thought of the book Carson had carried under the dining room table to read. "Maybe he's hoping his dad will be so impressed, he'll let him pick out a puppy." Carson had emphasized to Alix how important it was to begin with a puppy.

Beka popped into Robbie's brain again. *That's odd*, he thought, certain he hadn't called her to mind on purpose.

He raised a hand to block a sudden gust of blowing sand. Boy, the wind had really picked up. And it was hot. Must be the hottest day they'd had so far this spring.

Robbie tried to concentrate on the steps Carson

was taking to teach the dogs to fetch and return.

But images of Beka kept wiggling into his mind.

Why did he keep thinking about his sister?

The thoughts were coming stronger now. Closing his eyes, Robbie's mind formed such a vivid picture of Beka, it was hard to believe he wasn't looking at the real thing.

She was standing on a shore, somewhere near the lake.

And she looked frantic as she shouted his name. And Thatch's.

Was she all right? Why was she calling him? Did she need help?

And why had Thatch suddenly scrambled to his feet and started nuzzling him, yipping and whining with an urgency that said, *"We've got to find Beka. And fast!"*

16

A Ghost Who Hates Water

"Robbie!" Beka shouted. Out loud *and* inside her mind. "Thatch! Come here! I need you!"

Beka hopped off a craggy rock onto the muddy shore. Things weren't going well on her end.

Not only had Alix and Luka headed in the wrong direction, somehow they'd ended up at Danger Cove — *not* a good place to wander alone.

The path ran along a steep hillside, which dropped off sharply toward shore, where hidden rocks waited under shallow water.

The cove looked inviting the way it cut a smooth curve into the shoreline. But its innocent appeal was misleading. Danger Cove had earned its scary name.

In a matter of yards, the sandy lake bottom

ended at the edge of an underwater cliff. More than one swimmer had fallen into the deep pool and never been seen again.

Farther out, jagged rocks created a guessing game for boats trying to find a safe route to the pier.

When Beka followed Alix and Luka on their hike to the water's edge, she'd read every warning sign along the way. Like:

DANGER!

NO SWIMMING!

Alix didn't seem to notice the signs.

"This would be a good place to hide a few dogs," she told Luka, facing the gusty breeze, letting it whip her hair into tangles.

The same breeze kicked up whitecaps in the lake.

"How pretty," Alix said. "This is one spot I've never gone wading. And it's so hot today. Maybe I'll stop here and cool off a little."

Luka splashed into the water, almost as if inviting Alix to come in and play.

"Don't," Beka warned. "You're *miles* from the

dogs. And you're wasting time. This is no place to go wading — can't you read the signs?"

Alix pulled off her sandals and stepped into the water.

Then Luka did something strange. After exploring the first few feet of foaming water, she bounded back to shore, shook a gallon of droplets from her fur, and barked at Alix.

"What, Luka?" Alix called, splashing in the cove. "Come back in; it's nice and cold."

Luka barked again, racing up and down the shoreline.

"The cove isn't safe!" Beka shouted. "Even Luka knows that."

Alix ignored Beka's silent warning *and* Luka's noisy barking.

"*Please* don't make me come in after you," Beka murmured. "I *hate* water."

It all had to do with a long-ago canoe trip, getting dumped into the lake, and . . . Beka didn't like to think about that day. "If anything goes wrong, *I'll* have to rescue you — *me*," she added. "The ghost who hates water."

Watching Alix wade farther from shore made fear tighten Beka's chest. "Robbie! Thatch!" she screamed. "Please find us before it's too late!"

Dropping her voice, she added, "And before Danger Cove claims another victim. . . ."

91

17

A Quick Trip

Robbie scrambled to his feet. "Beka needs us. I'm not sure how I *know* she needs us — but she does."

He realized Thatch knew this already, and was trying to make him hurry up.

"But we don't know where Beka *is*." Robbie hustled to catch up with his dog. "She's probably *miles* from us."

Thatch became agitated. He raced toward the skiers' path, then back to Robbie, as if saying, *"Let's go! Somebody out there needs to be rescued!"*

"Maddie!" Carson barked. "Pay attention."

Maddie had sensed Thatch's dismay, and was trying to get to him.

"Stay!" Carson ordered, jerking on her chain.

Robbie wished he could snap his fingers, and find Beka in a matter of seconds. The wish reminded him of something that had happened to the twins once when they were on Mystery Island.

Feeling excited, he grabbed hold of Thatch. "Sit," Robbie told him.

But Thatch was in no mood to sit. He jumped up on Robbie with his front paws.

Robbie wrapped his arms around the dog as though the two were dancing. "This should work just as well," he mumbled.

Closing his eyes, he conjured up an image of his sister. "Think of Beka," he whispered to Thatch. "We want to be with Beka right now — wherever she is."

Robbie held on tightly, forcing his mind's eye to see his sister as clearly as if she was standing right next to him.

Beneath his arms, Thatch trembled, but stayed put, as if understanding what his master was trying to do.

In a matter of seconds, a foggy mist rose from the ground in narrow strands, which looked like bony fingers. The damp "fingers" grasped Robbie and Thatch, and lifted them off the ground.

Somewhere far away, Robbie heard a startled shriek, then dogs barking wildly.

The noise faded as the quiet mist rose higher and higher.

A minute or two passed.

The cloud set them on their feet (and paws) again. Slowly, it melted into the ground below Robbie's feet.

He had no idea where he was. Letting go of Thatch, he pivoted.

A few yards away, standing on the rocky shore of Danger Cove, stood Beka, mouth open, eyes gaping at him.

Robbie gave her a ghostly grin as Thatch dashed into her arms. "You called, madam?" he quipped.

Before Beka could answer, a scream shattered the silence of the quiet cove.

18
An Unbarked Code

"Alix!" Robbie shouted.

The twins raced to the edge of the water.

As Beka feared, Alix had waded out too far. Her last step came down on water instead of sand.

Deep water.

That, plus Danger Cove's infamous undertow made Robbie's shout come out as a breathy whisper. Not that Alix would have heard him anyway.

Thatch stood poised, one paw lifted, as if ready to fly to Alix's aid at a moment's notice.

Why was he waiting?

Robbie's answer came immediately.

Luka splashed into the water. In a heartbeat, she was swimming over the drop-off. Was Thatch holding back to let Luka rescue her own mistress? Was this an "unbarked code" between dogs?

Luka snagged Alix by the back of her shirt and dragged her toward land, dog-paddling as fast as her paws could go.

As soon as Alix's feet touched bottom, she pulled free from the dog and slogged her way to shore.

Dropping onto the muddy sand, she coughed and choked for a whole minute before recovering. Grabbing Luka, she hugged and kissed the dripping-wet dog.

"Looks like we weren't needed after all," Robbie said.

"Yes, you *are* needed." Beka fussed over Thatch since she hadn't seen him for twenty-four hours. "You *still* have to help me get Alix to the warming hut."

Quickly, Robbie's mind added, recalling Carson's mention of their last day of training.

His attention was drawn toward the dogs.

While Alix was busy wringing out her clothes and hair, Thatch was yipping at Luka. Luka stood stone-still, eyes and ears alert, aware that *something* was urging her to action. Something invisible. Like a ghost dog.

Thatch chased away from the cove toward the

path, barking until Luka caught up. Then he raced a little farther and waited for the other dog.

Alix brushed sand from her bare feet and stepped into her sandals. She clicked her tongue at Luka. "Let's go home, so I can change into dry clothes."

But Luka had absorbed Thatch's urgent message. No way was she going to let her mistress go home.

Dashing back to shore, Luka tugged at Alix's shorts, pulling her in the direction Thatch had gone.

"What is it?" Alix's face paled. She raced ahead, as though believing Luka had discovered Shawnee just around the bend.

Barking, Luka's instincts made her follow the invisible leader, stopping along the way to wait for Alix.

"Looks like *we* don't have to figure out a way to lead Alix to the warming hut at all," Robbie said. "Thatch will be our guide. Let's go."

"Okay, okay," Alix was saying. "Forget I'm soaking wet and chilled. At least I cooled off like I wanted to."

She hurried after Luka, wet hair flapping in the breeze. "If you think you know where Shawnee is, girl, then let's go get her."

19

The Scene of the Crime

Thatch and Robbie led the way, followed by Luka and Alix. Beka brought up the rear.

Robbie wished the mysterious cloud-fingers would lift the entire group and carry them back to the warming hut — but he doubted Alix would be willing to hold hands with a couple of ghosts and say good-bye to her body for a few minutes.

The hike was a long one. Alix moved slower and slower, complaining to Luka every mile or two.

"Do you know where you're going, girl?" she groaned. "You *act* like you do, but we've been hiking for hours."

An exaggeration, Robbie noted. More like *one* hour.

Beka whistled at him from the end of the line.

"Do you think it's wise for Alix and Luka to barge in on Carson?" she called. "I don't trust him."

Before Robbie could answer, Beka added, "If only she could see Carson and the dogs, without him seeing her. Maybe then she'd go straight to Mr. Tavolott — or the Shelbys — for help."

"Good point," Robbie called back. "Except Shawnee will probably go crazy when she picks up Luka's scent — which will tip off Carson. He'll know someone is spying on him."

As they neared the warming hut, barks and yips and shouts stirred the afternoon stillness.

Alix froze, listening. "Shawnee!" she yelped. "And Maddie?"

After complaining about being too tired to take another step, Alix flew into the last valley, stone-stepped over the stream while Luka (and Thatch) splashed through, then scrambled between trees up the hill.

The twins sped up in order to arrive at the hut ahead of Alix. The dogs were locked inside the hut, and there was no sign of Carson.

"Whew." Robbie felt relieved. "Now Alix can go for help without having to confront Carson."

The girl hit the skiers' trail at a dead run. She almost passed the warming hut before realizing that's where the barking was coming from.

"Shawnee!" she hollered, trying to get the door

open. "Oh, bother, it's locked. Who *did* this?" She yanked on the padlock in frustration.

Alix circled the hut, but couldn't figure out how to get inside. She kept mumbling comments about the *scene of the crime*.

Luka raised on her haunches to paw at the door. She seemed baffled. After finding her sister, why couldn't they get to each other?

Alix gave Luka's neck a good rubbing. "How'd you know Shawnee was here?"

"She had a little help," Beka said, answering for Luka.

"I can't get the dogs out by myself," Alix grumbled. "I need help." She scanned the area, as if getting her bearings to lead Mr. Tavolott's "posse" back to the spot.

Alix stepped close to the air vents. "Shawnee, I'll be back to set you free. Be a good girl, and I promise you extra crunchies for a whole week."

Shawnee whined in answer.

"And Maddie, if you're in there, I'll bring *you* crunchies, too."

Alix raced down the skiers' trail with Luka on her heels.

"Let's go," Robbie called to Thatch.

The dog was torn over whether to stay at the hut or go with them.

"Come with us, puppy," Beka urged. "We *need* you."

Need was an important word in the dog's "vocabulary." He vaulted down the trail after them, which made Robbie feel a whole lot better.

At the bottom of a steep hill, the trail cut southeast, which, Robbie knew, was the direction of the lodge. Following the trail was a roundabout way to go, but he didn't expect Alix to hike through the underbrush like he had earlier, and risk getting lost.

As minutes slipped by, the pounding of Alix's footsteps kept rhythm with the jingling of Luka's collar.

The twisty trail finally smoothed out. Alix's pace slowed by the second. Robbie could tell she was tired — not only from the long hike, but from her struggle in the water at Danger Cove.

Heading into a wooded glen, the girl rounded a bend and ran smack into — Carson!

"Uh-oh," the twins said in unison.

Thatch snarled at the boy, which Luka seemed to pick up on. Thatch's reaction must have subconsciously alerted her to danger. She acted unsure about how to greet him.

"Hi," Alix exclaimed, looking astonished at the coincidence of running into Carson again.

The expression on the boy's face was one of surprise and concern.

Robbie knew the concern had nothing to do with his collision with Alix.

"What are you doing all the way up here?" he asked, suspicion creeping into his voice.

"Well . . ." Alix tried to catch her breath. "My dog — my *other* dog — was stolen, and I just found her."

"You found her?" Carson's face crinkled in alarm. "Where?"

"Up there." Alix gestured in the general direction. "She's locked in a warming hut with other dogs."

"Other dogs?" Carson pretended to be innocently interested.

"I don't know how many there are. All that matters is that I've found them."

Carson blocked her way on the path. "What are you going to do about it?"

"Well, report it, of course." Alix gave him a puzzled look. "So the dognapper can be caught and I can get Shawnee back."

Carson was quiet.

Robbie could imagine his brain whirring like crazy, trying to figure out how to stop the girl from reporting the dognapper — meaning *him*.

"What if I helped you?" he offered. "I mean,

helped you get your dog back — not help you report it."

"Don't listen to him," Beka hissed. "He's trying to trick you."

Alix cocked her head and studied Carson's face.

Robbie could tell she was torn between the prospect of getting Shawnee back right away, and continuing her long trek into town to find help — then wait for the grown-ups to decide what to do.

"How can you help?" she asked. "The hut is padlocked."

"I know how to get it open," he answered without hesitation.

"No kidding," Robbie scoffed.

"You do?" Alix's voice sounded cautious.

"Sure." Carson headed up the trail. "Come on; I'll show you."

"Don't go. Don't go. Don't go," Beka chanted.

Alix gave a curious glance toward Luka.

"She's wondering why Luka's shrinking away from Carson," Robbie said.

"Listen to your dog," Beka told her. "She has a sixth sense."

"What's wrong?" Alix said, stroking Luka's head.

"Oh, she probably knows Shawnee is near," Carson explained.

"She knows *danger* is near," Beka snapped.

"*You.*" She pointed her finger at Carson. It disappeared into his chest.

Robbie couldn't help but chuckle at the confused shudder that visibly racked the boy.

Alix shifted from one foot to another, not quite convinced. "Well, I guess — "

"Come *on,*" Carson insisted, tugging at her arm. "You're wasting precious time."

"*Whose* precious time?" Robbie challenged. "Alix's or yours?"

To Robbie's dismay, Alix gave a *why not?* type of shrug, changed course, and followed Carson up the path, back to the *scene of the crime.*

20

A Terrible Job of Acting

"**W**hat *happened* to you?" Carson jabbed a thumb toward Alix's wet, wrinkled clothes as they hiked. "You look like you fell into the lake."

She glanced down as though the earlier incident had already been forgotten. Fiddling with her damp hair, she smoothed it into place, shooting him an embarrassed look. "I was wading at Danger Cove, and — "

"You went into the water at Danger Cove?" Carson's eyes grew as round as his glasses. "Wow."

She acted pleased that she'd impressed him. "Good ol' Luka here pulled me out."

"She did?" Carson looked even more impressed.

"What a cool dog." He reached to pet Luka, but she nipped at him and scuttled away.

"Lu-ka." Alix shook a finger at her. "Be good. You remember Carson from last night, don't you?"

"Oh, yeah," answered Robbie. "She remembers. But that was before Thatch warned her about him."

"So *that's* it." Beka snapped her fingers. "I wondered why Luka acted so unfriendly toward Carson. Do you think she and Thatch can *talk* to each other?"

Robbie watched the two dogs, trotting along side by side. "I don't think Luka sees him the way Maddie does. I think she just picks up on Thatch's thoughts. That's how she knew which direction to lead Alix, and how she knows Carson isn't to be trusted."

Twenty minutes later, the group climbed the last hill to the warming hut. "There it is," Alix whispered, pointing out the hut to Carson. "The dogs are locked inside."

"How do you know there's more than one dog?" Carson asked.

"Pu-leez," Beka scoffed. "Cut the act, Carson Tiller."

"I can *hear* them." Alix glanced at Carson as though he wasn't too bright. "I think the other

106

dog is Maddie. She belongs to the people renting the Zuffel house this week. They'd just gotten her as a wedding gift, and then she was taken."

"Yeah, but they have another dog to keep them company."

"No they don't."

Carson frowned at her. "They have *two* St. Bernards."

Robbie caught Beka's shocked reaction. "I knew it. He *did* see Thatch that night."

Alix returned Carson's frown. "No, they *don't* have two dogs," she insisted, absently wrapping Luka's leash around her hand. "And how do *you* know Maddie is a St. Bernard?"

Carson turned away, faking a sudden interest in a nearby cluster of wildflowers. "I saw the Shelbys once in town with their dogs."

"He's fudging," Beka said.

Now Alix was watching him as suspiciously as Luka. "So how are you going to help me get my dog back?"

Carson marched up to the warming hut and pretended to study the padlock.

"Aren't you afraid someone might be watching from the trees?" Alix called. "Standing guard?"

"Oh, yeah." Carson hunched his shoulders, looking side to side.

"He's a terrible actor," Beka groaned.

Alix moved closer, keeping a tight hold on Luka.

Carson peered at the lock. "Sure, I can get this off. It'll be easy."

"How?" Alix narrowed her eyes at him.

"I, um, read a book about picking locks."

"So. Do it. Pick the lock."

He hesitated. "I can't do it while you're watching."

"Why not? You said you'd *show* me."

He raised his arms in exasperation. "Look, I'm doing you a favor. Go around the hut and stand guard while I work on this."

Alix did what he asked. "Shawnee," she called softly. "I've come to get you."

Shawnee and Maddie started making so much noise, they sounded as though they were about to burst out of the hut in spite of the locked door.

Carson waited until Alix was out of sight, then whipped out a key and quickly undid the lock, shoving the key back into his pocket.

"There!" he exclaimed, unhooking the padlock. "That wasn't hard at all."

Alix rushed around the hut. "How'd you do it so fast?"

Carson acted like a hero as he pulled the door open.

Beka pretended to gag.

The dogs leaped from the hut. Shawnee jumped up on Alix; Maddie nuzzled Thatch. To the *unghostly eye*, however, it looked as though Maddie was nuzzling thin air.

"Come here," Carson said. "Look what's inside."

Alix shot a nervous glance toward the surrounding forest. "Shouldn't we get away from here *fast*? In case the dognapper comes back and catches us?"

"It'll only take a second," Carson said, disappearing inside.

Thatch and Maddie rushed in with him.

"They think he's going to feed them," Robbie said.

"Look," Carson called. "It's roomy in here and there's plenty of food and water for the dogs. Whoever did this must be a real nice guy."

"Ha," Beka said. "Don't flatter yourself."

Alix rolled her eyes. "Yeah, right, a real nice guy," she muttered, stepping into the hut. Shawnee and Luka dashed inside, too. Now it wasn't roomy anymore.

"It's terribly hot in here," Alix said, examining the hut.

Carson backed out to make room for everyone.

Then, before the twins realized what he was up to, he slammed the door and slipped the padlock back in place.

"Oh, no!" Beka cried.

The twins rushed forward, but there was nothing they could do.

Carson had caught them completely off guard.

"Hey!" Alix shrieked. "What are you doing?"

The boy hung his head. "I'm *really* sorry," he stammered. "But you gave me no other choice."

21
Tricked!

A chorus of barking shook the air.

Robbie hoped the wind would whisk the angry yipping down the valley to someone's ears. Someone who might call the police and report a strange disturbance in the foothills.

But the twins didn't have time to wait. The temperature in the now-crowded hut could reach a dangerous level, thanks to the afternoon's unrelenting heat.

"Why did you trick me?" Alix shouted.

An agitated Carson paced back and forth in front of the door.

"He's in *big* trouble now," Beka muttered. "How does he think he'll get away with this?"

"Alix," Carson called. "Please listen to me.

— I'm sorry you found the hut today. By this time tomorrow, I would have been finished."

"Finished doing what?"

Her voice sounded closer. Robbie assumed she had stepped up on the bench to get nearer to the air vents.

Carson sighed. "I would have been finished training the dogs."

"Go on," she told him, sounding confused.

"Remember when I told you my parents wouldn't let me get a dog?"

She didn't answer, so he continued. "Well, I thought my dad *might* let me get one for a pet if he could use it as a hunting dog. I wanted to prove I could train him a good bird dog."

Carson hunched on the ground in the shade to continue. "All I did was *borrow* Shawnee. I was going to give her back after I showed Dad how well I'd trained her. You still had Luka, so I thought . . . I thought . . ." He finished the sentence with a weak shrug.

"You thought Alix wouldn't mind sharing her dog?" Robbie finished for him. "Why didn't you just *ask* her if you could borrow Shawnee?"

"They didn't know each other," Beka reminded him.

"Then," Carson continued, "I worried about

112

Shawnee being here alone, so I borrowed Maddie for a few days. I really *thought* the Shelbys had another dog."

Alix was mumbling sarcastically, but Robbie couldn't hear what she was saying.

"Maddie is a quick learner," Carson added, talking fast, stumbling over his words. "My dad will be really impressed. He's bound to take me to the dog pound in Juniper to pick out a puppy."

"Poor guy," Robbie said. "He didn't *mean* to do anything wrong, yet he's getting himself in deeper by the minute."

"Poor *Alix*, you mean," Beka said, correcting him.

Carson looked as if he were about to cry. "Tomorrow's the day I'd planned to give my dad the demonstration. I was going to tell him the dogs belonged to my friends. . . ."

He let his voice trail off, waiting or hoping for encouraging words from Alix, but they didn't come.

"I'm so *close*, Alix. Let me do it. Don't ruin my plans — please?"

"No!" Alix's voice made him flinch. "You stole my dog. And Maddie, too. Now you've kidnapped *me*. And I'm supposed to sit here and let you get away with this?"

"But — "

"Carson, it's too hot in here for the dogs. They'll get overheated and — "

"One more day," Carson pleaded.

"NO!"

Sighing, he stood, brushed himself off, and headed down the trail, jabbering under his breath and shaking his head.

The sudden silence seemed strange after all the yelling and barking.

"Carson?" came Alix's trembly voice. "Please don't leave me here alone."

Her only answer was a bee, buzzing lazily around the air vents of the warming hut.

22
Surrounded by Ghosts

Robbie nudged Beka. "Are you thinking what I'm thinking?"

She grinned. "Is it time for another personal appearance? From the famous ghost twins of Kickingbird Lake?"

"And their ghost dog?" Robbie added.

"And their ghost dog," she echoed.

"*I* think so," he said. "It's going to get a lot hotter inside the hut. We'd better get them out *now*."

Beka agreed. "Thatch!" she hollered. "We need you! More than Maddie and Alix do right now. Come out, puppy!"

Above the yipping, they could hear Thatch's answering whine.

"Here, boy!" Robbie called. "Time to go!"

This time Thatch *smooshed* out of the hut so fast, Robbie blinked and missed it.

"You're an amazing *smoosher*," Robbie told him.

The ghost trio headed down the hill after Carson — who shuffled along uncertainly, head bowed, muttering how he *had to do it*.

Thatch and the twins quickly overtook the boy, stationing themselves ahead of him on the path.

"Think *visible*," Beka ordered, grasping Robbie's hand and placing her other hand on top of Thatch's head.

Thatch grumble-growled as Carson came nearer.

Was that the dog's way of making himself visible? Robbie wondered.

The twins stood in silence, focusing their thoughts on *being seen*.

Think *solid*, Robbie told himself, waiting for the heaviness to fall upon his shoulders.

And it did.

Quicker this time.

He felt as though he were sinking into the dirt on the pathway.

Glancing down, Robbie watched the imprint of his shoes begin to form in the sand. Moments later he couldn't see the imprint at all because his legs had lost their wispiness and were becoming solid.

"Nifty," he mumbled.

A terrified scream made him jerk his head up.

"You!" Carson rasped, pointing. "It's that dog again, and . . . and . . ."

Robbie hoped the boy would finish the sentence so he'd know *exactly* what it was Carson was seeing.

But the boy's face had gone ghost-white, and his legs were visibly shaking.

"W-what do you want?" His voice was so breathless with fear, they could hardly hear him.

"The key," Beka said, moaning the words. "We want the ke-e-e-e-y."

Robbie chuckled. She was trying to make her voice sound "ghostly."

"Gi-i-i-i-ve u-u-u-us the k-e-e-e-y."

"*What* key?"

"To the war-r-r-r-ming hu-u-u-u-ut."

"How? What? Why?" Carson's questions refused to come out. He backed away.

"He's going to make a run for it." Robbie kept his voice low so only Beka could hear.

Thatch hunched his back and inched forward, almost as if he were trying to act "ghostly," too.

Carson bolted into the trees.

"After him!" Beka shouted.

The boy ran recklessly, throwing desperate glances over his shoulder. Every time he tried to look behind, he'd run into a tree or bush he hadn't seen.

The twins couldn't have planned it any better.

Catching up with him was as easy as jumping into the lake without getting wet.

Thatch sprinted around the boy to block his way.

"Give us the key and we'll leave you alone," Beka called.

Carson came to a quick stop, gaping at the see-through animal barring his way.

Robbie dashed to the boy's right to keep him from running in that direction.

Beka stayed behind.

On Carson's left was a rock wall. He was completely surrounded.

By ghosts.

Panicked, he twirled, searching for an escape route. "D-don't hurt me," he wailed, falling onto his knees.

Robbie rolled his eyes. "Get up. We're not going to hurt you." After he said it, he wished he hadn't. If Carson *thought* he was in danger, he might do what they wanted.

Beka moved closer, holding out her hand. "Give us the key and we'll let you go."

"But — "

Robbie growled, trying to scare the boy into action. And to avoid an argument over the key.

Beka slapped both hands over her mouth to keep from laughing.

Robbie's growl worked on Thatch. Baring his fangs, he closed in on his prey.

Carson began to whimper. Shoving a hand into his pocket, he yanked out the key and flung it wildly toward Beka — without taking his eyes off the ghost dog.

The key sailed into the bushes before Beka could move to catch it.

"Gee, thanks," she muttered.

Beka was fading. Robbie noticed he could see trees behind her — or rather *through* her. Minutes before, he could not.

"Thatch!" Beka called. "Find the key."

Thatch dashed toward Beka, burrowing into the bushes.

Carson scrambled to his feet and backed away. He squinted, as if Robbie was fading, too.

Robbie bared his teeth and growled again, swiping pretend claws.

Carson bolted, stumbling down the wooded hill, crying for mercy.

Robbie chased after him, just for fun, howling,

"The Phantoms of the Forest strike again!" He wondered if Carson could hear him.

"Got it!" Beka cried, coming out of the bushes, hair straggling over one eye. She waved the key at her brother.

Raising one arm, Robbie brandished a make-believe sword. "Free the prisoners!" he hollered, scurrying back to the path.

His ghost posse followed.

At the warming hut, Robbie took hold of the padlock, concentrating until it moved in his hand. "Key, please?"

Beka handed it to him. Quickly, he unlocked the door, then hurled the padlock far into the bushes. "To keep Carson from doing this again," he explained to Beka's questioning look.

The door creaked open. The twins scuttled out of the way as the dogs leaped to freedom.

Alix peeked out cautiously, wiping her brow and gasping for cooler air.

Stepping outside, she turned, gazing suspiciously in every direction as though she knew this must be another one of Carson's tricks.

"Carson?" she called in a timid voice. "Did you change your mind?"

"No, he didn't," Beka said. "But we changed it for him." She bowed. "No need to thank us."

"Carson is long gone," Robbie told her. "You're

free, Alix. And you've rescued the dogs. Go be a hero and take Maddie home."

Alix must have been thinking the same thoughts. Pulling the wooden dog from her pocket, she gave it a big kiss.

"Maddie! Shawnee! Luka!" she cried, waving the lucky dog charm in the air.

The dogs (plus Thatch) danced around her as if they knew a celebration was in order.

"Let's go home!"

The group tore down the trail as fast as if they were being pursued by an invisible dognapper.

But they weren't.

It was only the local ghosts. Simply doing their job.

"All in a day's work," Robbie joked as the twins jogged down the trail toward home. "Right, Thatch?"

But before the words were out of Robbie's mouth, the ghost dog shot ahead, scrambling down the hill, desperate to catch up with his one true puppy love.

Epilogue

The highlight of the Shelbys' honeymoon was their happy reunion with Maddie. For the rest of the week, they didn't let her out of sight.

Alix came to visit every day, along with Shawnee and Luka. One time she even brought a few of her clients: Nikki, Cerise, and Leo.

Carson was grounded for the summer.

Mr. Tavolott "sentenced" him to three months of community service — at the Juniper Animal Habitat, helping to take care of all the animals.

And Thatch? Well, he hated saying good-bye to his new playmate, but Robbie and Beka promised to keep him so busy all summer that he wouldn't have one spare moment to miss her.

Rules to Ghost by

1. Ghosts can touch objects, but not people or animals. Ghost hands go right through them.
2. Ghosts can cause a "disturbance" around people to get their attention. Here are four ways: a) walk through them; b) yell and scream; c) chant a message; d) stand close enough to give them a *ghost chill*.
3. Ghost rules aren't always logical — rules of the world don't apply to ghosts.
4. Thatch's ghost-dog powers are stronger than ours. He can do things we can't. Sometimes he even teaches us things we didn't know we could do.
5. Ghosts can't move through closed doors, walls, or windows (but we can *smoosh* through if there is even one tiny hole).

6. Ghosts don't need to eat, but can if they want to.
7. Ghosts can listen in on other people's conversations.
8. Ghosts can move objects by concentrating until they move into "our ghost world" and become invisible. When we let go, the object becomes visible again.
9. Ghosts don't need to sleep, but can rest by "floating." If our energy is drained (by too much haunting or *smooshing*) we must return to Kickingbird Lake to renew our strength.
10. Ghosts can move from one place to another by thinking hard about where they want to go, and wishing it. It only works when Thatch helps us.

New Rules!

11. We can make people see us if we try hard to "think solid." It really *scares* people — but that's what ghosts are supposed to do!
12. The Ghost Leap: Helps us jump over tall bushes, wide streams, and huge rocks that are more than twice our height. Lets us move very quickly through forests and backyards.

Don't Miss!
The Haunted Campground Mystery —
Ghost Twins #6

"Rats," Beka mumbled, scowling at the black sky. She hated rain and she hated loud noises. For two cents she'd head back to camp — with or without Crash.

"Mrs. G.!" Crash whisper–shouted. "Please answer!"

But no one did.

Rain rapidly turned the dirt beneath their feet into slippery mud.

Suddenly a small animal, rushing for cover, darted across their path.

Crash shrieked. Turning, she raced *through* Beka, slipping and sliding. Her wild motions threw erratic flashlight beams into the branches.

THUNK!

Beka cringed, watching Crash reel from a blow to her forehead, then sprawl in the mud beneath the tree.

"Now what?" Should she wait for the girl to

wake up? Or go for help? "Crash is a good name for you," Beka told her.

Lightning and thunder struck again, making her uneasy. Lying under a tree in a thunderstorm wasn't the safest place to be. Besides, what if Crash had bumped her head hard enough to need a doctor? Waiting wasn't the right choice.

Beka sighed. Emergencies were much easier to handle when Robbie and Thatch were with her. "I'll be right back," she whispered to Crash. "Don't go anywhere."

She picked her way through the dripping trees toward camp. Then she remembered. Robbie and Thatch weren't there.

"I need help!" she shouted at the uncooperative sky. "Who's going to help me?"

The sky's unexpected answer was loud and abrupt, pushing Beka into a frantic run.

About the Author

Dian Curtis Regan is the author of many books for young readers, including *Home for the Howlidays*, *My Zombie Valentine*, and *The Vampire Who Came for Christmas*. A native of Colorado Springs, Ms. Regan graduated from the University of Colorado in Boulder. Presently, she lives in Edmond, Oklahoma, where she shares an office with a cat named Poco, seventy-six walruses, and a growing collection of "Thatch dogs."

Terror is watching.

High on a hill,
trapped in the shadows,
something inside a dark house
is waiting...and watching.

THE HOUSE ON CHERRY STREET

A three-book series
by Rodman Philbrick and Lynn Harnett

Terror has a new home—and the children
are the only ones who sense it—from the
blasts of icy air in the driveway, to the windows
that shut like guillotines. Can Jason and Sally
stop the evil that lives in the dark?

HCS1194

GET
Goosebumps™
by R.L. Stine

☐ BAB48352-8	#28	The Cuckoo Clock of Doom	$3.50
☐ BAB48351-X	#27	A Night in Terror Tower	$3.50
☐ BAB48350-1	#26	My Hairiest Adventure	$3.50
☐ BAB48355-2	#25	Attack of the Mutant	$3.25
☐ BAB48354-4	#24	Phantom of the Auditorium	$3.25
☐ BAB47745-5	#23	Return of the Mummy	$3.25
☐ BAB47744-7	#22	Ghost Beach	$3.25
☐ BAB47743-9	#21	Go Eat Worms!	$3.25
☐ BAB47742-0	#20	The Scarecrow Walks at Midnight	$3.25
☐ BAB47741-2	#19	Deep Trouble	$3.25
☐ BAB47740-4	#18	Monster Blood II	$3.25
☐ BAB47739-0	#17	Why I'm Afraid of Bees	$3.25
☐ BAB47738-2	#16	One Day at Horrorland	$3.25
☐ BAB49450-3	#15	You Can't Scare Me!	$3.25
☐ BAB49449-X	#14	The Werewolf of Fever Swamp	$3.25
☐ BAB49448-1	#13	Piano Lessons Can Be Murder	$3.25
☐ BAB49447-3	#12	Be Careful What You Wish For...	$3.25
☐ BAB49446-5	#11	The Haunted Mask	$3.25
☐ BAB49445-7	#10	The Ghost Next Door	$3.25
☐ BAB46619-4	#9	Welcome to Camp Nightmare	$3.25
☐ BAB46618-6	#8	The Girl Who Cried Monster	$3.25
☐ BAB46617-8	#7	Night of the Living Dummy	$3.25
☐ BAB45370-X	#6	Let's Get Invisible!	$3.25
☐ BAB45369-6	#5	The Curse of the Mummy's Tomb	$3.25
☐ BAB45368-8	#4	Say Cheese and Die!	$3.25
☐ BAB45367-X	#3	Monster Blood	$3.25
☐ BAB45366-1	#2	Stay Out of the Basement	$3.25
☐ BAB45365-3	#1	Welcome to Dead House	$3.25

Scare me, thrill me, mail me GOOSEBUMPS Now!

Available wherever you buy books, or use this order form.

Scholastic Inc., P.O. Box 7502, 2931 East McCarty Street, Jefferson City, MO 65102

Please send me the books I have checked above. I am enclosing $_____ (please add $2.00 to cover shipping and handling). Send check or money order — no cash or C.O.D.s please.

Name _____ Age _____

Address _____

City _____ State/Zip _____

Please allow four to six weeks for delivery. Offer good in the U.S. only. Sorry, mail orders are not available to residents of Canada. Prices subject to change.   GB894

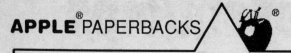

APPLE® PAPERBACKS

Pick an Apple and Polish Off Some Great Reading!

BEST-SELLING APPLE TITLES

- ☐ MT43944-8 **Afternoon of the Elves** Janet Taylor Lisle — **$2.75**
- ☐ MT43109-9 **Boys Are Yucko** Anna Grossnickle Hines — **$2.95**
- ☐ MT43473-X **The Broccoli Tapes** Jan Slepian — **$2.95**
- ☐ MT40961-1 **Chocolate Covered Ants** Stephen Manes — **$2.95**
- ☐ MT45436-6 **Cousins** Virginia Hamilton — **$2.95**
- ☐ MT44036-5 **George Washington's Socks** Elvira Woodruff — **$2.95**
- ☐ MT45244-4 **Ghost Cadet** Elaine Marie Alphin — **$2.95**
- ☐ MT44351-8 **Help! I'm a Prisoner in the Library** Eth Clifford — **$2.95**
- ☐ MT43618-X **Me and Katie (The Pest)** Ann M. Martin — **$2.95**
- ☐ MT43030-0 **Shoebag** Mary James — **$2.95**
- ☐ MT46075-7 **Sixth Grade Secrets** Louis Sachar — **$2.95**
- ☐ MT42882-9 **Sixth Grade Sleepover** Eve Bunting — **$2.95**
- ☐ MT41732-0 **Too Many Murphys** Colleen O'Shaughnessy McKenna — **$2.95**

Available wherever you buy books, or use this order form.